THE GHOST SQUAD

Mingling with the denizens of the underworld, taking their lives in their hands, and unknown even to their comrades at Scotland Yard, are the members of the Ghost Squad — an extra-legal organization answerable to one man only. The first Ghost operative detailed to discover the identity of the mastermind behind the buying and selling of official secrets is himself unmasked — and killed before he can report his findings to the squad. Detective-Inspector John Slade is his successor — but can he survive as he follows a tangled trail of treachery and murder?

GERALD VERNER

THE GHOST SQUAD

Complete and Unabridged

LINFORD
Leicester

First published in Great Britain

First Linford Edition
published 2017

A catalogue record for this book is available
from the British Library.

ISBN 978–1–4448–3277–8

1

Detective-Superintendent Gordon Hallowes, head of the Special Squad, known more popularly as the Ghost Squad, entered the office of the assistant commissioner of the C.I.D. at New Scotland Yard, wondering why that august individual had sent for him.

'Sit down, Hallowes,' said Colonel Blair from the other side of his big desk. He looked as neat and dapper as usual, but there was a slightly worried wrinkle between his normally smooth brows.

Hallowes, a big man with the bland, genial face of a country farmer, sat down in the chair facing the desk. The assistant commissioner passed a carefully manicured hand over his well-brushed grey head. He looked at a slip of paper on the blotting-pad in front of him, picked up a pencil and tapped thoughtfully with it on the desk. He said, after a slight pause: 'I've got a job for your bunch. It's a tricky job.'

Hallowes smiled. 'Most of the jobs that

come our way are, sir,' he said.

'Exactly,' agreed Colonel Blair. 'That's why it was decided to form the Special Squad in the first instance. You have unusual facilities.'

'Yes, sir,' said Hallowes.

The Special Squad was unique. It had powers that no other department in the C.I.D. possessed. Its job was to acquire information concerning the activities of criminals in a completely unconventional way. The small contingent of operatives worked in secret. They were unknown to the rest of their confreres at the Yard, and to the men on the beat and the local C.I.D. executives. They worked in the dark, the ordinary police departments taking over where they left off. They collected the evidence that would lead to the arrest of dangerous criminals, and they seldom appeared in court. Once they became known, their value would be gone.

They kept their identities a secret, working undercover in various guises but never appearing as what they were — police officers. They had a special office at Scotland Yard, though they seldom came there. There were no special hours of duty, no signing on and off. They worked at the job until it was satisfactorily completed, and then they reported to Hallowes by means of a special telephone number that was known only to themselves.

It was a lonely and dangerous job. They took their lives in their hands, for if they had once become suspected by the criminals among whom they lived, they would have received short shrift. But they were brave men, specialists in their particular job, and their successes since the formation of the squad had been remarkable.

'For some time,' continued Colonel Blair, 'we have become aware that there exists a new organization in the crime world. When I say organization, Superintendent, I do not mean the kind of organization so beloved of fiction writers. This is not a *fixed* organization in the accepted sense of that term. It is presided over by an unknown leader, certainly, but it uses any person or persons who may be useful. The members are, therefore, a kind of floating population. Do I make myself clear?'

'Quite, sir,' said Hallowes.

'These people,' went on the assistant commissioner, 'deal in secrets. A servant with a grudge who has found out something about his or her employer that is discreditable; an employee in a government office who has access to important secret documents; a member of a team engaged in nuclear fission experiments — all these people would find a ready and well-paid market for authentic information with this organization.'

'Blackmail?' suggested Hallowes.

Colonel Blair shook his neat grey head. 'Not exactly,' he answered. 'They do not use this acquired information *themselves*. They buy to sell — to the highest bidder. In the case of state secrets, to the agents of a foreign power — whichever foreign power is prepared to pay the highest price. In the case of information discreditable to an individual — and that individual would have to be someone very important in the sphere of politics — the services, or big business, to a *potential* blackmailer. It would have to concern a person or persons in the V.I.P. class. They don't deal in chicken-feed. So, you see, I don't have to tell you how very

4

dangerous this organization is.'

'No, sir,' agreed Hallowes. 'You want us to find out all about 'em? Who the people are who are working for the organization, and the man at the top?'

'Particularly the man at the top,' said Colonel Blair. 'Once we've got *him*, the rest of them would disintegrate, in my opinion. He's the brains. The others only do what they're told. Do you remember poor Fielding?'

'Detective-Inspector Fielding of Special Branch, sir?' asked Hallowes. 'He was found shot on a deserted stretch of road in the country —'

'He was,' broke in the assistant commissioner gravely. 'It was hushed up. We kept it out of the papers. Fielding had been working on this business for several weeks. He'd got very close to finding out the identity of the man at the top. He was a very efficient officer, poor fellow, but he had one drawback. He liked to keep things to himself until he'd completed his case. He never made any notes; kept all his information in his head. He was reprimanded for it once or twice, but it never made any difference — it was just his way, and he couldn't alter —'

'He was shot by this organization, sir?' said Hallowes.

Colonel Blair nodded. 'I don't think there's any doubt of it,' he declared. 'He was either shot where his body was found, or it was dumped there after he was dead. So, you see, you'll be up against a dangerous lot.'

'We're used to that, sir,' said Hallowes quietly. 'Can you give me any line that's likely to help?'

'I'm afraid not, Superintendent,' replied the assistant commissioner, shaking his head. 'You'll have to start from scratch. Fielding left nothing to show what he'd been working on. You'll have to be careful. These people'll be suspicious since the Fielding business. They'll be doubly on their guard now.'

Hallowes went back to his office, his bland, florid face wearing a thoughtful frown. The assignment was going to be a difficult one. But the Ghost Squad had been given difficult assignments before and brought them to a successful conclusion.

He hoped that this wasn't going to prove the exception.

He sat down at his desk, rested his elbows on his blotting-pad, and cupped his big face in his hands, pressing the tips of his fingers against his closed eyes. Slade would be the man for this job, he thought.

He reached for the telephone and asked the switchboard to connect him with a certain number ...

* * *

Detective-Inspector John Slade got out of the train at Clapham Junction, passed through the ticket barrier, and walked down the station approach. He was a man of medium height, with a lean, slightly hatchet-shaped face surmounted by thick brown hair that waved unobtrusively. He was dressed in a well-cut suit that showed signs of wear. There was nothing about him to suggest that he was a police officer. He looked like a superior clerk.

He came out of the station approach, turned to his left, and made his way in the direction of the high street. At a small shop that sold newspapers, cigarettes, and sweets, he stopped and went in. The middle-aged man in his shirtsleeves behind the counter was putting packets of tobacco from a cardboard carton on the shelves at the back of the counter. He smiled as he saw Slade. There was nobody else in the shop.

'Go straight through. The super's waitin' for you,' he said.

'Thanks, Weldon,' said Slade. 'I'll have a packet of Player's, please.'

Ex-Inspector Henry Weldon pushed a packet of twenty Player's across the counter. He had bought the shop when he had retired from the police force. It was a profitable little business, and the profits were augmented by the sum he was paid for the use of the back room as a meeting-place between Hallowes and his squad operatives. Here, the men and women who formed the Special Squad could meet for instructions in safety and secrecy. Weldon acted as the contact between them.

John Slade picked up his cigarettes and his change, went to the door at the back of the little shop, and passed through into a narrow passage beyond. There was a closed door further along the passage. At this he paused, tapped gently, turned the handle and entered. It was a bare room, shabbily but comfortably furnished with a couple of easy chairs, a table, a bookcase, and a square of worn carpet. Lounging comfortably in one of the chairs, smoking a pipe, was Hallowes.

'Come in, Slade. Shut the door and sit down,' said Hallowes. 'I've got a job for you.'

Slade shut the door and perched himself on the arm of the other chair. Opening the packet of cigarettes he had just bought, he took one out and lit it. 'What's it all about?' he said.

Hallowes repeated what Colonel Blair had told him earlier that day.

'I've heard rumours about this organization,' said Slade, when he had finished. 'Nothing definite, but rumours.'

'Well, now you can get busy and find something definite,' grunted Hallowes. 'It's up to you how you go about it. Of course, I'll give you all the help I can, but, as usual, you'll be on your own.'

Slade looked at the glowing end of his cigarette and wrinkled his forehead. 'It wants a bit of thinking out,' he said after a pause. 'The obvious thing to do, of course, is to pose as someone with something to sell. Do you know how these people with something to sell contact the organization?'

Hallowes shook his head. 'I know no more than I've told you,' he replied. 'You will have to figure the rest out for yourself. Maybe you can learn something from one of our snouts.'

'We've got to go carefully,' said Slade. He stubbed out his cigarette and lit another. 'If these people are suspicious because of the Fielding business, they'll be extra wary. They'll question the *bona fides* of any approach. Therefore, the character I assume has got to be foolproof. It's got to stand up to inspection.'

'Yes, you can't afford to fall down on that,' agreed Hallowes. 'Apart from the fact that I'd hate to lose an efficient member of the squad — and you'd be dead as mutton if they found you out — our chances of finding the man at the top 'ud go to odds on.'

'It's a pity Fielding kept so close about what he'd discovered,' muttered Slade.

'It's no good crying over spilt milk,' said Hallowes. 'Fielding was always like that. We've got to start from scratch. We know practically nothing. We've got to find it all out for ourselves.'

Slade got up and began to pace the floor. His brows were creased into a frown of concentration. Hallowes went on smoking in silence. After fifteen minutes, Slade stopped suddenly.

'I think I've got it,' he announced. 'You'll have to arrange my background, but this is how I propose to tackle it.'

He began to talk rapidly. He went on talking for the better part of an hour while Hallowes listened, interpolating a remark now and again. When Slade eventually finished, he nodded slowly.

'That's good,' he said. 'It's very good. I'll fix the background. As regards the woman, I'll arrange with Lydia. You'll get in touch with me here when you've got something?'

Slade nodded.

'Take care,' said Hallowes seriously. 'One slip and you'll be for it.'

'That's part of the game, isn't it?' said Slade. None knew better than he the risk he would be taking. From the time he assumed his new identity, he would be walking with death as a constant companion.

2

The Green Bottle stood on the corner of two bisecting streets in Soho. Its exterior was dingy and its interior only slightly less so. The spotted mirrors in their tarnished gilt frames that adorned the walls of the saloon bar were relics of the Edwardian period, and matched the faded hanging of once-red plush that time and dirt had reduced to a nondescript hue, difficult to identify. The marble-topped bar and tables were also relics of a bygone age, though some effort towards modernity had been attempted by the addition of a snack section to the bar, covered with a stained white cloth, which provided cold lunches during the daytime.

The Green Bottle, during the lunch-hour, was always full with businessmen, clerks, shopkeepers, and people who were employed in the immediate district, snatching a drink and a sandwich during the lunch-time break, or indulging more expensively in cold beef, potato salad, pickles, cold ham, pork, or such luxuries as their tastes, and pockets, dictated.

At night, however, the clientele was completely different. Gone were the businessmen, the clerks, and the employees from the district, to their various homes, their places taken by a heterogeneous collection comprising overly made-up, flashily dressed women from the streets; furtive-eyed men who kept a restless lookout around them as they drank; smooth-jowled, overdressed men with rings on their fingers and wads of notes in their pockets who talked among themselves in whispers as they sat at the marble-topped tables in little groups; a few tight-trousered, long-jacketed Teddy boys with their female counterparts — not many of these, as they preferred to congregate in the coffee-bars further up the street; and a few of the more or less respectable inhabitants of the district.

On a night when a thin fog made the street lamps bleary and the air damp and cold, a man entered the saloon bar, made his way to the counter, and ordered a double Scotch and soda. His gait was a trifle unsteady, and it was evident that the double Scotch was by no means the first he had consumed that night. He was a man of medium height, well-dressed in an expensive overcoat, with a silk scarf round his neck. His soft black hat was of good quality, and so were the pigskin gloves he carried. The other customers in the bar eyed him furtively as he drank, for he was a stranger among them, and they were suspicious of strangers.

A woman who would have been pretty if she had worn less make-up looked at him appraisingly. There was a half-smile on her overly red lips and an invitation in her dark eyes. The newcomer became aware of her as he finished his whisky and ordered another. Her glass was empty and, moving nearer to her, he said, speaking a trifle thickly and slightly slurring his words: 'Will you have a drink with me?'

'Thanks awfully,' she replied. 'I'll have a gin and lime.'

He ordered the gin and lime, put down a pound note, and pocketed his change. 'Happy days,' he said, taking a gulp from his glass. 'This is a pretty lousy place, isn't it? Do you come here often?'

She shook her head. 'I've never been in here before,' she replied. 'I was meeting a friend, but she didn't turn up.'

'Bit of luck for me she didn't, eh?' he broke in. 'If she had, you wouldn't've been here an' I wouldn't've met you.' He raised his glass. 'Here's to your friend that didn't turn up.' He swallowed the remainder of the whisky.

She laughed. 'You are funny,' she said, and took a sip of her gin and lime. 'What are you doing here? This isn't the kind of place to suit you. Were you meeting someone who didn't turn up?'

'No,' he replied. 'Just trying to pass the time. I don't know how I got in here. I was on my way to Piccadilly, as a matter o' fac'. Thought I'd like a drink an' saw this place. Bit o' luck again, eh? Let's have another drink.' He called for another double Scotch and a gin and lime.

'You've had quite a few tonight, haven't you?'

'Why shouldn't I?' he demanded sharply, swaying a little and gripping the bar to steady himself. 'What's it got to do

16

with you?'

'Oh, nothing,' she replied with a slight shrug of her shoulders. 'I didn't mean anything. There's no need to lose your temper.'

'If you had my life, you'd lose your temper too,' he said. 'You can't do anything these days without money ... That's what you want — money — lots an' lots o' money ... The on'y thing that's any use ... '

'You don't look as if you were hard up,' she remarked, eyeing him critically.

'I may not look it,' he declared, 'but I am. I'm damned hard up ... drowning in debts, that's me.' He had begun to raise his voice, which was growing thicker and more uncertain. A small man in a bowler hat and a raincoat who was quietly drinking a pint of draught stout nearby looked mildly interested. 'Drowning in debts,' repeated the other, shaking his head with the maudlin self-pity of the nearly drunk. 'Crushed down with 'em. You wouldn't believe it. Do you know, darling, if the people I work for knew my fi ... my finan ... my fianc'l position, I'd prob'ly get the sack?' He leaned forward and stared up at her, swaying back and forth.

'Who do you work for?' she asked curiously.

'Aha!' he said, wagging a finger at her. 'Aha, who do I work for, eh? Who d'you *think* I work for?'

'How should I know?' she said. 'I'm not a mind-reader.'

'You'd be shurprised. Important job I've got ... Whash your name, eh?'

'Lydia,' she answered.

'Mine's James — James Felton. Now, we're prop'ly in — introdushed.' He looked up into her face gravely, swallowed some more of his whisky, and went on: 'I like you, Lydia ... We could go plashes together, you an' I, eh? You're an un'shanding woman ... '

She laughed. 'What's this important job you do?' she asked.

'Gov'men' department,' he answered. 'Min'stry of Defensh... All very hush-hush an' top secret ... '

'You don't,' she said disbelievingly. 'The Ministry of Defence ... ?'

'You calling me a liar?' he demanded crossly. 'I tell you, I work for the Min'stry of Defensh ... Don't get paid much. Mis'rable pittance, thash all ... Thash why … always in debt. Lotsh o' people 'ud like to know what I know, eh? Lotsh o' people …' He had finished his drink. 'Letsh have another …' He fumbled in his pocket, producing a two-shilling piece and some odd coppers. 'Thash not much good, is it?' he said, shaking his head. 'Can't buy a drink with that … ' He pulled out a wallet from his breast pocket with difficulty, opened it, and searched in the interior. It was empty. 'Can't have another drink,' he said disgust-edly. 'No more money left … '

'You've had enough, anyway,' she said. She finished her gin and lime quickly. 'I must go. Thanks for the drink.'

'Here — jusht a minute,' he protested, clutching her arm as she was turning away. 'Jusht a minute. What about tomorrow night, eh? Get paid tomorrow … Meet me here an' we can go plashes … '

She hesitated for a moment and then she nodded. 'All right,' she said. 'I'll meet you in here at eight o'clock — if you remember.'

'I'll remember,' he answered. 'Shall be counting the hoursh … '

She laughed. 'See you tomorrow, then,' she said. 'Bye-bye.' She went out quickly.

The man, called Felton, stood swaying slightly at the bar after she had gone. He took out a packet of cigarettes, found there was only one left, put it in his mouth, lit it with great concentration, and flung the empty packet on the floor.

The quiet little man watched him with interest. For nearly a minute Felton stood smoking, his glazed eyes staring at the stained marble top of the bar. Then he turned and, staggering slightly, weaved his way between the tables to the door. As he went out, the quiet little man looked thoughtfully after him.

★　★　★

At eight o'clock the following evening, the saloon bar of the Green Bottle presented much the same appearance as it had done on the previous evening. A number of the customers who had been there on the former occasion were absent, but their places had been taken by others of a similar type. The quiet little man in the bowler hat and raincoat occupied his previous place by the bar, and was engaged with the crossword puzzle in an evening paper over his pint of draught stout. Outside a drizzle of rain was falling, but the fog of the night before had dispersed.

It was a few minutes after eight when James Felton came in. He gave a quick glance round, went over to the bar, and ordered a double Scotch and soda. The little man looked up from his crossword at his entrance, but almost immediately went back to it again.

Felton drank his whisky quickly and ordered another. There was no sign of Lydia. Twenty minutes past eight, half-past, and she had not put in an appearance. The little man finished his stout and ordered another. He folded his paper and put it in the pocket of his raincoat. He looked speculatively at Felton.

'Your friend not turned up yet?' he remarked pleasantly after a moment or two.

'Apparently not,' said Felton. 'Perhaps she thought I wouldn't. I was a bit under the weather last night.'

'I know,' said the little man.

'You were here, were you?' asked Felton. The little man nodded. 'I heard you make the appointment,' he said. 'Maybe she thought you wouldn't turn up, an' again maybe she thought it wasn't worth comin'.' He came nearer, bringing his stout with him. 'You was a bit talkative, you see, an' you ran out o' money. These women are all the same, you know. They're only interested in a man with money.'

'That applies to most people,' said Felton a little bitterly 'Money's the only thing that counts, isn't it?'

'It helps,' agreed the little man. 'You can do most things if you've plenty o' money, can't you?'

'You're right there,' said Felton. 'It isn't so easy to come by these days — especially if you get a fixed salary. By the time they've deducted tax, and you've paid your living expenses, there's precious little left over.'

'There's a lot o' people making money, though,' said the little man. 'Heaps of it. It depends what sort o' person you are, I suppose. You can always make money — if you're not too particular how you make it.'

'Can you?' said Felton. 'I wish I knew how. There's not much I wouldn't do to make money — real money. But it's the right opportunity that counts. That's not so easy to come across.'

The little man laughed. 'People who think like that usually land up in clink,' he remarked. 'What with one thing an' another, it's difficult to make money honestly — a lot of money. There's always the pools, of course.' He drank some of his stout and took out a cigarette case.

'Have a drink with me?' suggested Felton, but the other shook his head.

'No thanks,' he said, lighting his cigarette. 'I've had my quota for this evening. By the way, I'd like to give you a word of advice, if you won't take it the wrong way.'

'What is it?' asked Felton.

The little man came closer and lowered his voice. 'I wouldn't talk quite so much, if I were you. About your job, I mean. I don't know whether it was true or not — maybe you were just trying to impress that woman last night — but ... well, I'd be a bit more careful, if I were you. You don't know who might be listening.'

'What did I say?' asked Felton a little uneasily.

The little man in the bowler hat told him.

'Did I say that?' demanded Felton. 'Good Lord, I must have been high. It's all true, of course. I do work in the Ministry of Defence, and a number of very confidential documents come under my inspection.'

'I shouldn't say so much about it,' said the other. 'I don't want to seem impertinent, but I thought you were being a bit indiscreet, if you know what I mean? There's a lot of the wrong people who might be interested.'

'I'm glad you told me,' said Felton gratefully. 'I don't remember much about last night.'

'When the drink's in, the wit's out,' said the little man. 'It's none o' my business, of course. Thought I'd give you the tip, that's all.' He nodded pleasantly and went out.

James Felton ordered another whisky and soda and stood at the bar drinking it slowly. The little man's remarks seemed to have made him thoughtful. After another half-hour and two more whiskies, he bought a packet of Player's, lit one and left the Green Bottle.

It was still raining, but he ignored the drizzle and walked slowly in the direction of Piccadilly Circus. He bought an evening paper from a man outside the Underground station, and thrusting his hand into his overcoat pocket to find the loose change to pay for it, found a piece of paper which he was quite certain had not been there when he left the public house.

Tucking the newspaper under his arm, he entered the Underground station, found a spot that was out of the way of the stream of people hurrying to and fro, unfolded the paper, and read the message that had been scrawled on it:

'If you really want money, go to Martin's Garage at the corner of Greer Street tomorrow night at ten. Ask for Mr. Snow.'

That was all, but it sent Mr. James Felton home considerably happier than he had been before.

3

Ex-Inspector Henry Weldon was weighing out some toffees for a small child when Slade entered the shop the following morning. 'Go on through. I'll be with you in a minute,' he said, nodding in the direction of the door at the back. This was a polite fiction that he adopted whenever there happened to be anyone else in the shop, no matter who it might be.

Slade opened the door and made his way to the room where he had met Hallowes before. The superintendent was occupying the same chair and smoking the same pipe. He might never have moved since the other interview. 'Well,' he greeted, 'what have you got to tell me?'

Slade sat down and lighted a cigarette. 'I think I'm on to something,' he said.

'Good,' grunted Hallowes. 'Lydia said she hoped you didn't have too bad a hangover.'

Slade grinned. 'I didn't feel too good

the next day,' he confessed. 'I must've got through quite a lot of whisky. Lydia was grand. She played up wonderfully.'

In some subtle way, Slade had shed the character of Mr. James Felton. His appearance hadn't altered very much. The line of his eyebrows was different and his hair was brushed differently, but it was in his general expression that the change lay. James Felton possessed rather a weak face, whereas John Slade's was strong and forceful.

'So the idea paid off, eh?' said Hallowes, puffing at his pipe. 'Tell me about it.'

Briefly, Slade explained what had happened on the two visits he had paid to the Green Bottle.

'Do you think this man in the bowler hat and raincoat who got into conversation with you last night is the contact?' asked the superintendent.

'I don't know,' said Slade. 'He may be. He certainly didn't put that message in my pocket; that was done on my way to Piccadilly. It was damned clever. I've no idea who put it there.'

'Some little dip could've done it,' remarked the superintendent. 'It's not really important. The important thing is this appointment at Martin's Garage for to-night.' He frowned. '"Ask for Mr. Snow." H'm. I wonder who he is.'

'Another contact, I expect,' said Slade. 'You can bet your life that the top man is well-hidden in the background. These people are clever. That fellow in the bowler hat, for instance. If he *is* one of them, there's nothing to connect him with anything criminal.'

'If they hadn't been clever, we'd have had them before now. You'll have to go carefully. Your background's all right. There's a James Felton working for the Ministry of Defence and he's been put wise to you. That's just in case they try and check on you. You'll have to go to the office every morning and leave in the evening. But there's a back way that you can slip in and out of as you wish. Your flat has been looked after, too. Ostensibly, James Felton has been living there for the past two years. I think we've taken care of everything our end. The rest is up to you.'

'I know,' said Slade with a wry grimace. 'Well, I'll do my best. I've a feeling that life is going to be a bit hectic from now on. I'll report here at intervals or through Lydia.

There's a chance that I may be tailed. If so, I'll ring up Lydia and adopt the teashop routine.'

'That would be the best way,' said Hallowes. 'I should keep away from here. These people aren't going to risk taking you on your face value, you know. They dare not. Whatever happens tonight, you'll be closely watched. Work through Lydia or leave a message with Weldon. Is there anything else?'

'There's one other thing,' said Slade. 'The reason these people have contacted me is obviously because they imagine that, due to the nature of my supposed job, I'm in the position to supply them with valuable information — secret information. Right?'

Hallowes nodded. 'And you want some kind of fake information that you can offer?' he said.

'Yes,' agreed Slade. 'I suggest that it should be something to do with the redistribution of rocket bases.'

Hallowes took out a small notebook and jotted down a reminder. 'I'll attend to that. I'll have a fake document on those lines sent to your flat — or better still, you can pick it up at the Defence Ministry. Anything else?'

'I can't think of anything at the moment,' said Slade after a moment's thought.

'Well, I wish you the best of luck,' said Hallowes. 'And don't forget — take care … '

⋆ ⋆ ⋆

Martin's Garage, on the corner of Greer Street, was a small and outwardly unpretentious place, as Slade discovered when he arrived there just before ten o'clock that night. Pausing on the other side of the street, he took stock of it with interest. There were two petrol pumps and a pull-in for cars. An attendant in a soiled white coat was making some kind of adjustment to one of the pumps when Slade crossed over and accosted him. He was a young man with reddish hair and a smear of black oil down one cheek.

'Mr. Snow?' he repeated in answer to Slade's question. 'Ain't never 'eard of 'im. We ain't got nobody of the name 'ere.'

'Are you quite sure?' persisted Slade.

'Course I am,' said the attendant. 'Never 'eard the name afore. You must've got the

30

wrong place, mate.'

Slade frowned. Had they got suspicious and called the whole thing off? Were his efforts, that had seemed so promising, going to peter out into a dead end?

'There isn't another garage with the same name near here, is there?' he inquired.

The red-haired youth shook his head. 'No, this is the only one, mate,' he declared.

Slade was considering what to do next when a car came round the corner and pulled up in front of the petrol pumps. A fattish face was thrust through the open window of the driver's seat and a slightly hoarse voice called out: 'Put in a coupla gallons, will you?'

The attendant went over to the nearest pump and coiled the hose.

'Do you happen to be Mr. Felton?' asked the man in the car, eyeing Slade questioningly.

'That's right,' replied Slade. 'Mr. Snow?'

'Snow it is,' said the man in the car. His fat face creased into a sudden grin so that his small black eyes almost disappeared in folds of flesh. 'Hop in.'

Slade came round to the other side of the

car, opened the door, and got in beside the man in the driving-seat.

'Won't be a jiffy,' said Mr. Snow.

'I found a note in my pocket,' said Slade. 'I don't quite know what it means but I thought I'd come and find out.'

'That's right, chum,' said Mr. Snow. 'You'll find out all about it.' He paid for his petrol and drove away.

'Where are we going?' asked Slade.

'Not far,' answered Mr. Snow, skilfully avoiding a taxi and turning into a side street. 'If you want to make a bit of extra money, now's your chance.'

'How?' demanded Slade.

'He'll tell you that,' answered the fat-faced man.

'We're going to see someone?' asked Slade.

The other chuckled. 'Well, not exactly,' he answered. 'Best not ask too many questions, chum. You'll see.'

They turned into another side street and pulled up about halfway along it on the right-hand side.

'Out you get,' said Mr. Snow, opening the door nearest him and sliding from under the wheel. Slade got out. Mr. Snow came round the back of the car and joined him on the pavement.

'This way,' he said, and walked a few yards up the narrow street. In front of a closed shop, he stopped, took a key from his pocket, and approached the door. Slade saw that it was a small and rather dingy-looking shop. In the window were a number of carnival masks and a couple of wax figures of the kind used to display dresses.

The fat man opened the door of the shop and ushered Slade inside. There was a musty smell mingled with the odour of wax. Dummies of varying kinds filled the small space, and the walls were hung with papier-mâché masks, some plain and some painted; hideous and grotesque faces that leered out of the gloom.

Mr. Snow relocked the door. 'Queer place, this,' he said. 'Always gives me the creeps. Like a waxworks show. Sometimes you could swear the dummies move.'

He went over to a door at the back of the shop and opened it. Slade saw that it led into a large, bare room that seemed to be a kind of workshop. Here there were dummies in all stages of manufacture, some without heads, some with heads but no arms or legs. On shelves stood a collection of heads, as though this were some hitherto undiscovered Bluebeard's chamber, and every available space that was not occupied by dummies, or portions of dummies, was filled with masks. The whole effect was indescribably eerie.

'Well, here we are,' remarked Mr. Snow. 'I'll leave you now. Good luck!' He grinned, went quickly over to the door by which they had entered, and disappeared. Slade heard him cross the floor of the shop beyond, and the opening and shutting of the street door.

He was alone.

With all his senses alert, he waited, looking about him a little uneasily. In the semi-gloom — for the only light came through a dirty window in the side wall and probably had its source in a nearby street lamp or electric sign — the place was almost macabre. There was scarcely any sound, although he thought he could hear the faint strains of dance music from somewhere beyond the window.

What was going to be the next move?

He had been brought here to meet

someone. The head of the organization? Was he coming here? Slade's nerves were tensed with expectancy. Surely it wasn't going to be as easy as all that?

What happened was so unexpected that he almost jumped from the shock. There was a slight click, and then out of the gloom, coming apparently from nowhere, a voice addressed him. 'Good evening, Mr. Felton,' it said.

It was a queer voice — an unreal voice. There was something altogether inhuman about it. Slade felt a momentary creeping of the flesh.

'I apologize for this somewhat melodramatic method of communication, Mr. Felton,' continued the disembodied voice, 'but I assure you that it is necessary. You can speak quite normally. I shall hear you.'

Slade cleared his throat. 'Who are you?' he asked. 'Why was I brought here?'

'Your first question, I'm afraid, must remain unanswered,' replied the voice. 'Your second question you can answer yourself. I am given to understand that you are in financial difficulties. Is that correct?'

Slade had located where the voice came from now. It came from somewhere high up in the wall of the room. There must be a concealed loudspeaker, and also a concealed microphone that picked up his voice.

'Supposing I am?' he answered. 'What then?'

'I may be in a position to help you,' said the voice. 'If you are in urgent need of money ... '

'Who told you I was in urgent need of money?' demanded Slade. 'It's true enough, but how did you know?'

'I hear things. I make it my business to hear things.'

'How can you help me?' asked Slade. 'Are you a money-lender?'

'No, I don't lend money. But if you have anything of value to sell, I am prepared to pay a good price — in cash.'

Slade laughed. 'So is anybody,' he retorted. 'It's easy enough to get money for value received.'

'Not for the sort of thing I imagine you might be prepared to offer, Mr. Felton,' broke in the voice.

'I've nothing of value.'

'But you are in the fortunate position of being able to get it. You work in the offices of the Ministry of Defence.'

'What's that got to do with it? I shan't be working there long if my present financial position leaks out.'

'There is no reason why it should. You must have access to certain information of a secret nature — information that would be worth a considerable sum of money ... '

'Are you suggesting that I should sell government secrets?' demanded Slade with just the right tinge of indignation in his tone. 'What are you, a spy?'

'I am a businessman,' answered the voice. 'I hope that you are too. I have shown you a way by which you can make money without a great deal of effort. If your scruples are such that you would prefer to remain in your present state of — er — insecurity, that is your affair. I would point out, however, that a word to the department you work for, disclosing your present unfortunate financial state, might result in you finding yourself in an even more unfortunate one.'

'You would do this unless I agree to what you suggest?' said Slade. 'That's precious near blackmail.'

'It *is* blackmail,' retorted the voice calmly. 'Let us not split hairs, Mr. Felton. Come, now. What are you going to do?'

Slade was silent for a moment. He didn't want to appear too eager. He felt that Felton wouldn't have jumped at the suggestion at once. However desperate and unscrupulous he might be, the prospect of turning a traitor to his country for money would certainly go against the grain.

'Well?' said the voice impatiently.

'Supposing I did have something to sell,' said Slade cautiously. 'How would I contact you?'

'You wouldn't,' answered the voice. 'We would contact you. When you have information you wish to dispose of, you will go to a newsagent's shop in Greek Street. The name is Samson. You can't mistake it. There is a board outside displaying advertisements. You will have the following advertisement put on the board: "For Sale. Child's teddy bear. Good condition." The charge for a week will be sixpence. Is that clear?'

'Quite,' said Slade.

'Samson's has no connection whatsoever with us. It is an ordinary newsagent's and tobacconist's. But the card will tell us that you have something to sell, and we will get in touch with you. If what you have is worth money, you will be paid according to its value to me. Is that understood?'

'Yes,' said Slade.

'Good night,' said the voice. 'We shall look for the card.'

'I haven't decided — '

'You will. You can leave by the street door to the shop. Good night, Mr. Felton.'

There was another faint click, and Slade realized that the interview, if it could be called that, was over.

He took out a packet of cigarettes and lit one. The simplicity of the whole set-up almost staggered him. It was brilliant. So far there was nothing to connect any of the people with whom he had come in contact with each other, or with the organization. Who the man was who had spoken over the loudspeaker, he hadn't the remotest idea. He rather thought that no other member of the organization had either. He could have been a fair distance away when he spoke.

Slade thought that he was probably using a two-way radio similar to the ones in the police cars. This had been connected to a loudspeaker instead of a telephone.

He would have liked to stay and have a good look at the dummy and mask shop, but he decided that it might be watched. There would be another opportunity sometime when they didn't know he was there.

He made his way out of the workshop, through the outer shop, to the street door. It had a Yale lock. Slade turned the knob and the door opened. As he closed it behind him, the lock clicked. As simple as that.

He walked thoughtfully through the back streets into Shaftesbury Avenue. He had got somewhere, anyhow. If he had not seen the top man of the organization, he had spoken to him. It was a step forward in the job he had undertaken. But there was a long way to go before he discovered the identity of the man he was seeking. He would take every precaution to remain unknown.

But, Slade thought, he had done a lot in a short time, and he had been lucky. He hoped that his luck would continue to hold.

4

Slade allowed nearly three days to elapse before he made the next move in the game. During that period he became aware that the organization were taking no chance on him. He heard that somebody had telephoned the Ministry of Defence inquiring for James Felton, and he came home to his flat one evening to discover that the place had been carefully searched. Little evidence had been left behind of the intruder's presence. Only a man of Slade's experience could have known that anything had been touched, but he had taken certain precautions for just such an event as this, and the signs were obvious to him. It was lucky that there was nothing in the flat that did not support the character he had adopted.

He was followed, too. It wasn't always the same man, but he knew he was being tailed. He had expected this and was prepared. When he left the offices on the evening of the third day, he went to Greek Street and put a card bearing an advertisement for a child's teddy bear in the board outside Samson's, the newsagent's and tobacconist's. A man in a camel-hair coat and a soft hat, who had trailed him before, followed him from the offices to Greek Street. Slade wasn't sure whether he had followed him home or not, but later that evening, when he cautiously looked out the window, he saw the man pass slowly under a lamp-post in the street below. A continuous watch was, apparently, being kept.

The fake document concerning the distribution of the new rocket bases had arrived from Hallowes. Slade made a careful copy of it, putting the original under the carpet in his sitting-room. It would never do to part with that. The unknown head of the organization was sufficiently sensible to realize that James Felton would never risk stealing the original, as its loss would be discovered almost immediately. He would expect a copy. But would he be satisfied? Slade decided that he would take the original with him as well as the copy. He'd explain that he had done so to prove the copy's authenticity, but that he must return it to the office at once. That would do the trick and help to establish his *bona fides*. He wanted this to be the beginning of a series of transactions between himself and the organization. Each one would give him a greater chance of discovering the identity of its unknown leader.

The letter reached him on the morning following the appearance of the advertisement card. It was only a half-sheet of cheap paper in a cheap envelope. The fact that it was correctly addressed proved, if proof were needed, that he had been watched. The card had merely stated 'inquire within'. The envelope was typed, and so was the brief message inside. It ran: *Be outside the Prince's Theatre tonight at 9.30.*

That was all. Another car pick-up, thought Slade. Where would they go this time? The shop of the dummies and the masks? That seemed scarcely likely, otherwise the meeting would have been arranged at the shop. After all, he had been there before, so there was no point in secrecy. No, this was probably some fresh rendezvous. They seemed to be adept at covering their tracks.

When he left the office that evening

shortly after half-past four, having slipped in through the back entrance ten minutes previously, he made his way to a small tea-shop in a side turning off the Strand. It was one of those 'help yourself' places that had sprung up like mushrooms since the last war. There were not a great number of people there. Slade picked up a tray from the pile near the entrance to the pen where people were forced to move behind, like the herded sheep which they seemed to have become, and selected a cake and cup of tea, helped himself to sugar and a spoon, paid the bill at the other end, and carried the tray over to a vacant table.

After a little while, a woman came in. She took her tray and helped herself to tea and cakes. As she carried her tray in search of a table, she caught sight of Slade. 'Why, Mr. Felton,' she exclaimed in surprise. 'Fancy seeing you in here. Can I bring my tray to your table?'

The expression on Slade's face was one of slight annoyance. 'If you wish, Miss Adams,' he said without enthusiasm. 'I shall not be staying very long. I just came in for some tea.'

'How funny. So did I,' said the woman as she set down her tray. 'Isn't it strange that we should have chosen the same place?'

Out of the corner of his eye, Slade saw that a man had followed her in. It was the same man whom he had seen pass under the lamp-post outside his flat. So he was still under observation. Lydia, although no one would have recognized her for the flashy-looking woman he had picked up in the Green Bottle, sat down.

'It's been a simply *dreadful* day,' she said, removing the things from the tray. 'I've never made so many mistakes. I don't know what *can* have been the matter with me.'

The watcher had secured a cup of tea for himself and was seated at a nearby table reading a newspaper.

'Some days are like that,' remarked Slade. Under his breath and without moving his lips, he said: 'Be careful, we're being watched.'

'Oh, I know, Mr. Felton,' she answered. 'It's just one of those things, isn't it?' In the same manner that Slade had adopted, she added: 'The man with the newspaper?'

Slade gave an almost imperceptible nod.

'I thought the day would *never* end,' went on Lydia brightly. 'Do you ever find days like that, Mr. Felton?'

'Very frequently,' replied Slade. 'I think most people do.' Almost in the same breath, and with no visible movement from his lips, he said: 'Nine-thirty — outside the Prince's Theatre.'

'I'm going to a dance tonight,' said Lydia. 'My boyfriend is taking me. He's ever such a nice boy — you know, looks really smart. Not like most of the boys you see today. Treats you properly, too …' With barely a pause, she said: 'Do you want a cover?'

'No,' he answered in the same almost inaudible tone. 'They might spot it.' In his normal voice, he said: 'I hope you have a very pleasant evening, Miss Adams.'

'Oh, I always do with Gregory — that's his name, Gregory. It's not a very common name, is it?'

'I suppose it isn't,' he said. Under his breath, he added: 'I'm going now. See if you can tail that fellow.' He rose to his feet.

'Oh, are you going, Mr. Felton? I was so enjoying our little chat.'

'I'm afraid I must. Good night, Miss Adams. Have a good time.'

'Thank you,' she answered. 'I shall have to hurry too. I've got to change.'

He gave her a brief smile and left the tea-shop. Hallowes would get the latest information from Lydia. The tea-shop routine, with variations, was one they had used before to pass on information.

On the way to his flat, Slade kept a sharp lookout for his trailer. Sure enough, the man was following him. Slade tried to spot Lydia, but he failed to see any sign of her.

* * *

At eight o'clock that evening, a man turned into the street containing the shop of dummies and masks. Slade, had he been there, would have recognized the man called Mr. Snow. Reaching the door of the shop, he took a key from his pocket, unlocked the door, and stepped quickly inside. Closing the door behind him, he made his way through the shadowy shop, with its eerie atmosphere, to the workroom beyond. Glancing at the watch on his wrist by the dim light from the window, he saw that he was early. The man he had come to talk to would not be available yet.

Mr. Snow found a chair, sat down, and lit a cigarette, smoking thoughtfully. Except when there was somebody who had something to sell to the organization, he was the only contact with the man at the top. Even so, he did not know his real identity. From the disembodied voice over the loudspeaker he received his instructions, and he made his reports to it. He was quite happy with the arrangement. He was well-paid and he took very little risk.

He had nearly finished his cigarette when a slight click warned him that the man he had come to talk to was there. 'Are you there, Snow?' asked the voice.

'Yes, I'm here,' answered Snow. 'The report on Felton is satisfactory. I've had his flat searched. There was nothing to show that he isn't what he seems. He's been trailed consistently and we've found nothing suspicious. He *did* meet a woman in a tea-shop this afternoon ...'

'By appointment?' interrupted the voice.

'No,' replied Mr. Snow. 'Stringer, who

was trailing him, says that it was by accident, and Felton didn't seem to be too pleased at having his tea interrupted. She apparently works in the same department as Felton. Her name's Adams. They were only together for a few minutes and then Felton left.'

'Where did he go?' asked the voice.

'Back to his flat,' said Snow. 'Stringer is watching the place now. He'll trail him to the Prince's Theatre.'

There was a short silence. Then the loudspeaker came to life again. 'It sounds all right,' said the voice. 'But we can't afford to take any risks — not after that Special Branch man. He seemed genuine on the surface. You'd better take every precaution. I wonder what he's got to sell.'

'We shall know tonight, I suppose,' said Mr. Snow.

'Yes,' agreed the voice. 'I hope it's something worthwhile. We've gone to a lot of trouble over Felton.'

'It should prove to be very well worthwhile,' said Snow. 'It might prove to be a gold mine, if he continues. He's in a position where he could get hold of a great deal of valuable information.'

'Yes, Felton might very well turn out to be one of our most profitable finds,' said the voice. 'Is there anything else you want to tell me?'

'Not at the moment.'

'Very well. Contact me through the usual channel if you've anything further to report.' There was a click. The interview was over. Mr. Snow got up. He went through into the shop, opened the street door, emerged into the street, and shut the door behind him.

Two streets away, a man in a small car parked by the kerb closed a panel over a compartment under the dashboard which contained the radio installation through which he had been speaking, and drove slowly away.

★　★　★

It wasn't a very pleasant night. The rain had stopped, but there were signs that it was only temporary. The lights under the canopy of the Prince's Theatre gleamed on the wet pavement. The red light from the neon sign over the frontage was reflected in the roadway. There were few people about, and not many cars passed. It was the dead hour. Later, when the cinemas and theatres broke, there would be a great deal of activity as the pleasure-seekers came pouring out to make their various ways to their respective homes.

Slade arrived at the spot he had been told in the note, five minutes early. Lighting a cigarette, he waited idly, staring at the huge poster along the side of the theatre opposite. There was a season of ballet. In the frames under the portico, he could see photographs of scenes from some of the season's offerings, together with other photographs of the principal dancers. One or two taxi cabs, the light on the front showing that they were for hire, slowed hopefully as they passed him.

It was exactly at nine-thirty that a large car swung out of Shaftesbury Avenue and pulled up in front of him. A man leaned out the window of the back seat. 'Get in,' he said curtly. He opened the door, and Slade got in beside him. Almost before the door was shut again, the car moved forward. Slade saw that the man beside him and the driver were the only other people in the car.

He saw something else. Resting on the lap of the man who had invited him into the car was a small automatic. The fingers of one of his gloved hands were curled down the butt. The man saw the direction of his eyes, and laughed harshly.

'Don't try any tricks,' he said. 'We know all about you.'

Slade's heart sank. Had he had all his trouble for nothing? Had his real identity been discovered? Had he made some slip that had given him away?

'I don't know what you mean,' he said nervously, still keeping to his character of James Felton and trying to behave as he imagined that mythical gentleman would do in these circumstances. 'I was told to be where you picked me up at nine-thirty. I don't know what you mean by "tricks".'

'Don't you?' interrupted the man beside him unpleasantly. 'Well, it'll be all the better for you if you don't.'

'I have a valuable document to sell,' said Slade. 'I didn't expect a hold-up. I expected a fair deal —'

'You'll get a fair deal,' said the other.

'Where are we going?' asked Slade.

'Don't ask questions,' snapped the man with the automatic. 'If you wait, you'll see.'

'I only wish to say,' said Slade, 'that I refuse to deal with anyone except the principal person concerned in this matter.'

'Let me tell you,' said the man beside him, 'that you're not in a position to dictate who you'll deal with. You'll do as you're told, understand?'

'I strongly resent your attitude,' said Slade.

'Maybe you do,' said the other, 'but there's nothing you can do about it, is there? Now, just shut up.'

Slade did so. He was coming to the conclusion that the other had been bluffing when he said that they knew all about him. It was probably a trick to make him give himself away if he had been anything other than what he pretended to be. Perhaps it was a method that they adopted with everybody, just as a precaution. He began to feel less doubtful.

They passed through London and out into the suburbs. Slade recognized Hammersmith, Richmond, Kingston. They came to Esher and presently out into open country. Halfway along a deserted stretch of road with fields on either side, the man beside him gave a curt order to the driver, and the car stopped.

'Get out,' said the man, and Slade obeyed.

The driver joined them as they stood in the drizzle of rain that had started to fall.

'Search him,' snapped the man with the automatic.

'Now, look here — ' began Slade indignantly.

'Be quiet,' broke in the man. 'Go ahead.'

The driver, with the expertise of a man who was used to the job, made a thorough and systematic search of Slade's pockets, the lining of his jacket and overcoat. If there had been anything concealed, he would have found it. But there wasn't. Slade had been careful to ensure that he was carrying nothing that wasn't in keeping with the character of James Felton. He even carried a medical card in that name.

They were interested in the long envelope in his inside breast pocket that contained the fake documents — the original and the copy. The man with the automatic examined it carefully.

'You be careful of that,' said Slade. 'It's secret and valuable information that I hope to dispose of to your principal. If I'd known that there was going to be all this fuss, I wouldn't have — '

'Here you are,' said the other, giving him back the envelope. His tone was less harsh. 'You've passed, so far, with a clean bill.' He turned to the driver. 'All right,' he continued. 'Get back in the car. We've finished.'

The driver went back and climbed into the driving-seat. Slade was going to get in the back when the man with the automatic stopped him.

'Not you,' he said. 'You stay here.'

'Look here,' said Slade angrily, 'this is ridiculous. You bring me all this way, search me, and now you're going to leave me stranded — '

'You won't be stranded for long,' retorted the other. 'Just wait where you are. Don't move.' He stepped into the car and it drove swiftly away.

Slade watched the red tail-lights disappear in the wet darkness. Well, that was that.

What was the next move going to be? These people obviously took endless precautions. They made quite sure that their own safety was completely ensured. No wonder the organization had so far continued to evade the efforts of the police to discover much about it. Fielding, he thought as he waited in the rain, must have got as far as this. His body had been found by the side of a stretch of deserted country road similar to this. He must have disclosed his hand too soon and been shot for his hardihood.

He, Slade, would have to be more careful. He would have to penetrate the various layers of precautions that protected the identity of the top man until he had discovered, without any possibility of doubt, who he was. When he had acquired irrefutable evidence of his identity, the police could move in and finish the job. But he must be very careful not to make any premature move. The big fish could easily slip through the net if he made a mistake.

The headlights of a car appeared in the distance. Slade stiffened. Was this what he was supposed to be waiting for? The car lights drew nearer, slid past him, and stopped. A muffled voice called to him from the open window of the driver's seat, and Slade went over to the car.

He could barely see the muffled figure behind the wheel, but it looked bulky — the figure of a big man enveloped in a thick overcoat — and the face was completely concealed by a mask that covered it from eyes to chin.

'You are Felton?' asked the muffled voice.

Slade admitted that he was.

'You have something to sell — what is it?' said the man in the car.

Slade produced the envelope. 'It's a list of the new rocket sites,' he explained. 'There's going to be a redistribution. It's top secret.'

'Let me see it,' said the man. He put his hand, which was gloved, through the window. Slade withdrew the two documents from the envelope and gave them to him.

The masked man flicked on the light of an electric pencil torch. Spreading the documents on his knees, he sent the tiny light searching back and forth across the typewritten lines. He read rapidly. 'This seems all right,' he commented. 'One of these is a copy of the other?'

'Yes,' explained Slade. 'The original must go back before it's found to be missing. I brought it to prove the authenticity of the copy. The copy is all I can sell you.'

'It is sufficient,' said the masked man. 'You did well to bring the original. I would not have dealt with you on the copy only. Remember that in the future.'

'The future?' echoed Slade. 'Do you expect me to be able to do this kind of thing often?'

'I am hoping so,' said the masked man. 'We are wasting time. I'll give you two hundred pounds for this.'

'Two hundred!' expostulated Slade. 'But that would be worth thousands in the right quarter —'

'Two hundred,' interrupted the other firmly. 'You can take it or leave it.'

'Can't you make it a thousand?' said Slade. 'I expected at least that amount.'

'Then you were optimistic, my friend,' said the masked man. 'My expenses are heavy. I have to find the right market. Two hundred is my offer.'

'It's no good to me,' declared Slade firmly. 'It won't get me out of my trouble.

I must have at least a thousand to square my creditors — '

'I suppose you realize,' broke in the other harshly, 'that I could have got these from you for nothing? My men could have taken them when they searched you. You couldn't have done anything about it.'

'I expected a fair deal,' said Slade sullenly.

'You're getting one,' snapped the masked man. 'Now, listen to me. You may be worth quite a lot to me. You have access to other important secrets. I'll stretch a point in your case. I'll give you a thousand — in cash — now ... '

'Thanks,' said Slade.

'But,' went on the other, 'you've got to continue working for me. You understand?'

Slade felt a sudden surge of elation stir inside him. There was nothing he wanted more. This was what he had hoped for. 'You mean join the organization?' he asked.

'Yes,' answered the masked man, 'but you will continue to live as you do now. You will only contact us when you are told.'

'I'm willing,' said Slade.

'Very well.' A gloved hand reached towards him. It held a thick pad of notes.

Slade took the packet as it was thrust through the window of the car.

'There's five hundred there,' said the unknown. He produced a second wad of notes and passed them over. 'Here is another five hundred.'

Slade stowed the two thick packets away in his overcoat pockets.

'There's one thing I would like to say to you,' continued the masked man. 'Don't try at any time to become curious concerning me. You will only be wasting your time. Nobody knows me. The person who ever does will never be in a position to profit by his knowledge.'

'I'm not of a curious disposition,' said Slade.

'That is just as well,' said the other. 'You will be receiving a small camera with a supply of microfilm. Use it in future. There is too much risk in taking away the actual documents. Somebody might decide that they wanted them in a hurry. It would be unfortunate if they were not there.' He said no more, but the car began to move forward.

'How do I get back?' asked Slade, moving

along with it.

'That is your business,' retorted the man in the driving-seat. The car gathered speed and vanished in the darkness. Slade stood in the rain, which was now falling heavily, and looked after it. He had tried to get a glimpse of the number but it had been covered.

He took out a cigarette and lighted it. He hadn't the least idea where he was, and it was anything but pleasant standing about in the rain. He turned and started to walk back along the deserted stretch of road. There was quite a considerable distance to cover before he could hope to find anything in the nature of transport to take him back, but the prospect failed to depress him.

He had succeeded tonight in making contact with the unknown head of the organization. It was true that he knew no more about him than he had before, but it was a further step in the right direction.

5

Lydia followed the man in the camel-hair coat and soft hat when he left the tea-shop, keeping sufficiently in the rear to avoid him suspecting her. There was no doubt he was tailing Slade, though he appeared to have no idea that he was himself being tailed. He never even once glanced back, but kept steadily behind his quarry until Slade reached his flat.

Lydia expected that he would remain watching the entrance to the flat, but he quickly showed that such was not his intention. After hesitating for a moment on the pavement, he turned away and began to retrace his steps. Lydia was pretending to ring the bell at a house further along the street as he passed by, and a few seconds later was following in his wake.

At the end of the street, he stopped and looked up and down the main road. Lydia guessed that he was seeking a taxi, and her heart sank. Unless she was lucky enough to find one, too, she would lose him.

After a little while, an empty cab appeared and the man in the camel-hair coat hailed it, gave a brief instruction to the driver, and got in. The cab drove off, and Lydia looked desperately up and down the street. There wasn't another taxi in sight. And then, just as she was prepared to give it up as a bad job, a taxi, its illuminated sign on the front showing that it was for hire, came round the corner behind her. She ran towards it and pulled open the door.

'Follow that cab — the one that's passing the cinema,' she said, and prayed that the driver wouldn't argue. She was lucky. He nodded, winked, and as she scrambled inside, swung the cab round in pursuit.

Although the taxi with the man in the camel-hair coat had had a good start, they quickly caught up with it. The driver of Lydia's cab evidently knew his business, for a few yards behind the other taxi he slowed down and kept behind it as it presently crawled through the West End traffic. They negotiated the roundabout at Piccadilly Circus and turned into Shaftesbury Avenue, swung round into Wardour Street and from thence into Frith Street. In front of the entrance to a restaurant, the cab in which the man in the camel-hair coat was travelling drew in to the kerb and stopped.

Lydia tapped on the window of her taxi and the driver pulled up. She got out and thrust a ten-shilling note into the man's hand.

'Doin' a double-cross on yer, is he?' said the driver with a knowing grin. 'Well, I 'opes yer catch 'im out.'

He drove away, and Lydia walked slowly past the restaurant which the man in the camel-hair coat was just entering. The name over the fascia was outlined in neon tubing, as yet unlighted, and she made a mental note of it: the Eldorado. From the glimpse she caught of the interior as she passed the glass swing doors, it appeared to be both modern and expensive. It was unlikely, she thought, that the man she had been following had gone there for a meal. It was too early for dinner, and the only light in the place was in the vestibule, which seemed to indicate that it was not yet open.

She walked to the end of the street, turned, and slowly came back again. This time she stopped and looked at the framed photographs of a woman in a very low-cut and tight-fitting evening gown that adorned the entrance. There were several of these in various poses bearing the inscription: 'Vanya, the Girl with the Golden Voice'. Evidently Vanya was one of the attractions the Eldorado offered its customers with their dinner. The question was, was the man in the camel-hair coat connected with the restaurant, or had he merely called there?

Lydia crossed over the road and looked in a small hat shop. There was a mirror at the back of the window, and she could see the front of the restaurant reflected in it. There was no sign of the man returning. It was going to be difficult to watch the place for long. She would be getting conspicuous if she lingered. Perhaps the best thing to do would be to report to Hallowes.

She waited for a little while longer and then walked slowly away. She decided that at least the Eldorado was worth a closer inspection.

★   ★   ★

Salvatori, the manager of the Eldorado, sat in his office smoking a cigarette. It was a special brand of Egyptian tobacco that he had specially imported. He was a short, dapper man with an almost completely bald head and a thin streak of black moustache that lay across his upper lip like a caterpillar. He was immaculately dressed in evening garb, with a white carnation in his buttonhole, and he exuded a faint aroma of aftershave lotion of the most expensive brand. Everything about Salvatori was of the best.

Nothing second-rate or cheap was allowed to intrude into his life, and yet he looked far from happy as he stared at the virgin blotting-pad in front of him. His brows were contracted into a frown and his lips were pursed into a discontented pout. The fat, beautifully manicured and beringed hand that held the oval cigarette trembled slightly.

Emile Salvatori was a greatly worried man.

He would have given a great deal to have been able to extricate himself from his present position, but he was in too deep to be able to hoist himself out without more danger than his rather craven soul could face. Greed had got him in, and fear held him there with the sucking tenacity of quicksand.

The telephone buzzed softly. Nothing so blatant as a bell was allowed to disturb the serenity of the office. Salvatori stretched out his hand and picked up the receiver. At the sound of the voice that came over the wire, his face changed.

'Listen,' said the voice curtly, and Slade would have recognized it for the voice of the unknown man in the mask shop. 'There is something that must be done — at once.'

Salvatori listened, and the expression on his face became more and more worried as the toneless voice proceeded.

'Does it 'ave to 'appen 'ere?' he asked, and his accent was more pronounced than usual. 'Can't it be arranged some other way?'

'Are you questioning my orders?' inquired the voice. The unknown had not raised it, but the quality had suddenly become steely. 'This is urgent.'

'Yes, yes,' said Salvatori. 'I understand the urgency. I am not questioning your orders, but — '

'Then see that it is done,' interrupted the voice.

'It shall be done as you say,' assured Salvatori hastily, and the phone went dead.

He put down the receiver, took out a silk handkerchief, and wiped his face. The flesh had sagged, and he looked grey.

He was still sitting and staring at the blotting-pad when the door opened and the man whom Lydia had followed entered. He was no longer wearing the camel-hair coat but was dressed in a well-cut dinner suit.

'Well,' he began, and then catching sight of Salvatori's face: 'What the hell's the matter?'

'Everything is the matter,' replied Salvatori. He crushed out his cigarette in the big cut-glass ashtray. 'You will not be pleased at what I have to tell you, Clint … '

He repeated the telephone conversation he had just finished. Clint listened, his face expressionless. He was a thin, dark-featured man with a long, narrow jaw and a tight-lipped mouth. His eyes were a curious light blue that gave him, in some lights, a queer illusion of blindness.

'Tomorrow night,' he said when Salvatori had finished. 'During Vanya's first number. Why does it have to be done here, in the restaurant?'

'I asked that,' said the manager, 'but ... ' He shrugged his shoulders. 'You know how it is. 'E won't listen to anything. 'E gives the orders and expects them to be carried out.'

'It'll be easy,' said Clint. 'The lights are dimmed.'

'There must be other ways,' grunted Salvatori. 'It could 'ave been arranged somewhere else. But no — it 'as to be 'ere.' He got up, went over to an elaborately fitted bar in one corner of the office, selected a bottle of Hennessy, and poured out a liberal quantity of brandy. 'I 'ope nothing goes wrong,' he said, cupping the glass in his hands and sniffing the bouquet from the contents. 'I shall be glad when it's over.' He drank a little of the brandy and carried the remainder back to his desk.

'Don't I get a drink?' asked Clint.

Salvatori made a gesture. 'I'm sorry,' he said.' 'Elp yourself.'

Clint did so. 'You worry too much,' he said, squirting a little soda into his brandy.

'You must be getting squeamish in your old age.'

'You say that, eh?' retorted Salvatori. 'Do you not see that we take all the risks? 'E is safe. Nobody knows 'im. For us it is different. We carry the babies.'

'You're losing your nerve,' sneered Clint.

Salvatori took a gulp of the brandy. 'If that is all I lose,' he said, 'I will be 'appy.'

* * *

'I think this place might be worth looking into,' remarked Superintendent Hallowes, staring into the bowl of his pipe thoughtfully. 'Yes. Now, suppose you an' Slade have an evening out, eh?'

Lydia looked dubious. They were sitting in the little room at the back of Weldon's shop on the morning following the day that she had tracked the man in the camel-hair coat to the Eldorado.

'They know Slade,' she objected.

'They know him as James Felton,' said Hallowes gently. 'That's all the better. Why shouldn't he be spending some of the money they've paid him by taking a woman out for the evening? It's natural. Of course, you'll have to change your appearance. I'd get another operator, but you've seen this man. It'll be better if you go.' He tapped the ashes from his pipe and began to methodically refill it from a capacious pouch.

'I suppose you're right,' she agreed. 'When do we go?'

'Why not this evening?' said the superintendent. 'There's no point in wasting time. You may not discover anything, but on the other hand you may. We've just got to follow up every line. I'll tell Slade to book a table. He'll be phoning me here this morning. You'd better get in touch with me about lunch-time and I'll tell you all the arrangements — where you meet him an' what time.'

Lydia got up. From the tone of Hallowes's voice, she knew that the interview was over. 'All right,' she said. 'Anyhow, I'll get a good dinner.'

'That's right,' said Hallowes. He smiled. 'You know what I always say in this job? Never miss a meal if you can help it. It may be your last.'

* * *

The Eldorado was fairly full when Slade and Lydia were shown to their table by an obsequious waiter. It was not a very large place, but the decorations were pleasantly subdued and the lighting was discreet. There was nothing blatant about the Eldorado. Everything was in the best possible taste, and the food was excellent. Slade, as he glanced down the menu, concluded that at the prices, it should be.

'What would you like?' he inquired. 'It all goes down on the expense sheet, so don't stint yourself.'

Lydia — no one would have recognized her as the woman of the Green Bottle, or the woman who had met him in the tea-shop — looked up from the menu she was consulting. 'I'd like melon,' she said, 'and some roast duckling with orange sauce, green peas and sauteed potatoes. We might finish with crepes Suzette.'

'The bill for that little lot ought to entitle us to a share in the place,' said Slade. 'Would you like a cocktail?'

A wine waiter had appeared by the table with a wine list and an ingratiating smile. Lydia considered for a moment. 'Yes,' she said. 'I'd like a Bronx, please.'

'I'll have a double pink gin,' said Slade. 'See that there's not too much pink and that the gin is Plymouth.'

The waiter bowed. 'You would like to order wine?' he asked.

He opened the list and laid it gently in front of Slade. Slade looked down the list and ordered a Châteauneuf-du-Pape '52. The waiter bowed again and glided silently away. He was replaced by another waiter almost instantly, who took the order for the dinner. A junior waiter set a basket of rolls on the table.

Slade offered Lydia a cigarette, lit it for her, and took one himself. He looked leisurely round. Next to the table at which they were sitting was a good-looking Jewish man with a pretty blonde woman in a lilac dress, in the low corsage of which she wore a spray of orchids. The dark man had just made some kind of humorous remark, for the woman was laughing. Near to them sat an elderly man with grey hair with a woman of about the same age. They appeared to be arguing over something on the menu. It was a very polite argument, conducted quite good-humouredly, but neither was giving way to the other.

The muted chattering of voices made a pleasant background, interspersed with the tinkle of a glass and an occasional burst of soft laughter. There was a piano on a raised dais near a curtained alcove, and this, Slade concluded, was used for accompanying Vanya, the Girl with the Golden Voice, when she appeared.

'Can you see the fellow you followed?' he asked in a low voice, leaning towards Lydia. 'He might be among the waiters.'

She shook her head. 'I've been looking,' she answered in the same tone. 'I haven't seen him yet.'

Slade finished his pink gin. In spite of the number of waiters in the place, the service was slow, he thought. Perhaps the fault lay in the kitchen staff. The criticism had scarcely drained from his mind when the melon arrived, and was almost instantly followed by the wine waiter with the bottle of Châteauneuf-du-Pape, which he opened with great ceremony after graciously allowing Slade to inspect the label, and poured a small quantity into his glass.

Slade indicated that it was to his liking, and the waiter filled Lydia's glass and his own, carefully stood the bottle on the table, bowed, and withdrew.

'You haven't told me yet how you got home last night,' said Lydia, sprinkling ginger over her melon from the shaker.

In a low voice, Slade related his experience after keeping the appointment outside the Prince's Theatre. 'I was lucky to get a lift back,' he ended. 'A chap in a car took pity on me, but by that time I was pretty wet.'

'You've no idea, I suppose,' she said, 'what the man in the car was like — I don't mean the one who gave you the lift.'

'I know the one you mean,' said Slade, and he shook his head. 'No, he wore a mask which covered the whole of his face. The voice was the same as the man's in the mask shop. They take infinite precautions, these people. It's not going to be easy to trap them.'

'I think you've done pretty well so far,'

remarked Lydia. 'You've succeeded in getting into the enemy's camp, which is something.'

'But not enough. I've got to find out the identity of the King Pippin. I may need you to help me there.'

'How?' she asked. 'This melon's delicious.'

'If I was paying for it out of my own pocket,' said Slade, 'it 'ud choke me. I'll tell you how you can help, when the time comes,' he added. 'At one of these interviews with our unknown friend, he's got to be followed. I can't follow him because I'm on the wrong end. There's got to be someone who can pick him up when he leaves, after the interview is over, and find out where he goes. Then we've got him.'

'Do you think he'll use the mask shop again?' she said.

Slade shrugged his shoulders. 'I don't know,' he replied, 'but I should think it's more than likely. It's obviously been used before. The set-up has been carefully prepared. I've asked Hallowes to find out who owns it. It's a genuine business, I think.'

He broke off as two waiters arrived with

the roast duckling and all its trimmings. When they had been served and the waiters had gone, Slade took a sip of the wine and continued: 'This place must be quite near the shop. In fact, I should imagine it backs onto it.'

'Which makes it all the more likely that it's used in conjunction,' said Lydia. 'It was a good thing I managed to follow that man.'

'It certainly was,' agreed Slade. 'You get full marks for that.' He looked in the direction of the piano. A young man in evening dress had just come through the curtained archway and taken his seat at the instrument. 'Now, I suppose, we're going to have Vanya?'

'What a pity,' said Lydia. 'I shan't be able to concentrate on the lovely meal. They really ought to time her appearance better.'

There was a preliminary chord on the piano and the lights began to fade, leaving only the dimly shaded lamps on the individual tables. A spotlight from somewhere in the roof focused on the curtained archway. A voice — Slade couldn't see whence it came — broke into the sudden silence. 'Ladies and gentlemen,' it announced sonorously, 'we have great pleasure in presenting — Vanya!'

The piano began the prelude to a blues number, there was a moment of expectancy as though everyone in the restaurant had held their breath, and then the curtains covering the archway parted, and Vanya stepped through. She was dressed in a skin-tight gown of white satin, the bottom of which ended in a wide flare, and in her night-black hair she wore a single white rose. There was a burst of applause, which died quickly as she began to sing.

The song was nothing — it was the singer that made it. In a deep and slightly husky voice that seemed to hang throbbing in the air, the words took on a mournful meaning that swept over the silent audience and played on their emotions like fingers on the strings of a harp. The lyrics were banal, the music ordinary, but the artistry that put the number over was touched with genius.

And then, in the midst of the second refrain, it happened.

There was a slight flash in the beam of the spotlight, and Vanya's voice broke into a choking cry. The white of the satin gown was dyed red as she swayed for a second, then crumpled forward against the side of the piano and slid to the floor of the dais.

'Lights!' cried a voice from the shadows. 'Put up the lights!'

A woman screamed, and there was a babble of excited voices. A short, stout man with an almost bald head came quickly from the back of the room. Slade and Lydia were on their feet, trying to see what was happening. The dark man at the next table with the blonde woman was cursing softly but fluently.

'I am a doctor.' A tall, thin man forced his way to the dais. 'Please don't crowd round.' He bent down over the crumpled heap that had been Vanya, and his examination was brief. 'This woman is dead,' he announced. 'She has been stabbed!'

The bald man — it was Salvatori — raised his arms in a gesture of despair. ''Ow could she 'ave been stabbed?' he cried excitedly. 'No one was near 'er!'

'There's the knife,' broke in the doctor. 'It must have been thrown.'

The flash he had seen in the beam of the spotlight, thought Slade.

'It is terrible — terrible!' wailed Salvatori. 'The reputation of this restaurant will be ruined. ''Ow could such a thing 'ave 'appened?'

The doctor eyed him coldly. 'You'd better send for the police,' he said curtly. 'It was murder.'

6

Divisional Detective-Inspector Mason stood in Salvatori's office and gently rubbed his chin. In the restaurant below, his sergeant and the divisional surgeon were busy with the almost endless routine that accompanies an investigation into wilful murder. The photographer and fingerprint man was going about his job methodically, oblivious of the excited and chattering crowd that still filled the place.

On Mason's orders, no one had been allowed to leave. This included Slade and Lydia. So far as the inspector was concerned, they were ordinary customers. It was part of the regulations of the Ghost Squad that its operatives were, and remained, unknown to their confreres in the Metropolitan Police.

'This woman was killed by someone who threw a knife,' said Mason.

'Who could 'ave done such a thing?' demanded Salvatori, spreading his plump hands. 'It is shocking! Who would want to kill 'er?'

'That's what I'm trying to find out,' said Mason. He wasn't very impressed with what he had seen of the manager of the Eldorado. 'Did you see anything that might help us?'

Salvatori shook his head. 'Nothing — I see nothing — nothing at all,' he declared.

'No one seems to have seen anything,' grunted Mason.

'It will ruin me,' cried Salvatori. 'All the publicity ... Why did she 'ave to be killed 'ere?'

'Most inconsiderate of her,' said the inspector. He turned to the swarthy man who had been seated at the next table to Slade. 'Did you see anything, sir?'

'No. It was so unexpected,' he replied. 'And the lights were very dim. I saw nothing.'

'I doubt if we shall find anyone who did,' said Mason pessimistically. 'In the dark it would have been easy for someone to throw that knife. You were the dead woman's agent, I believe?'

'That's right,' said the dark man. 'My name's Barney — Rodney Barney. I run

Barney's Variety Agency in Greek Street. I got Vanya the booking here.'

'Do you know of any reason why someone should want to kill her?' asked Mason.

Barney shook his head. 'None,' he said. 'She was a nice person.'

'Someone didn't think so,' grunted the inspector. 'How long was she employed here?'

'The contract was for a month,' said Barney. 'There was talk of an extension.'

'I see. What did you know about the dead woman, Mr. Salvatori?'

'I know nothing about her,' said Salvatori. 'I engage 'er as an artiste, that is all.'

'I see,' said Mason again. 'Well, it seems to be a queer business. Had she any relations?'

'She never mentioned any,' answered Barney. 'She had a flat in South Kensington, I believe. That was the address I have in my books.'

'Did she live there alone?' asked the inspector.

'So far as I know,' replied the variety agent. 'I knew very little about her private life.'

He gave Mason the address, which the

inspector wrote down in his notebook. 'There's no further information that either of you can give me?' he asked. 'Nothing that might help us to find the murderer?'

'I 'ave told you everything I know,' declared Salvatori untruthfully. 'It is a terrible thing. Why should anyone choose my restaurant to kill this woman, eh? It is not sensible. There must have been other opportunities.'

'Maybe — maybe not,' said Mason. He decided that he didn't like Mr. Salvatori, who appeared to be chiefly concerned with the effect that the murder would have on his business. 'Well, that's all for the present. I shall probably want to see both you gentlemen again.'

'I'll come down with you,' said Barney. 'I've a lady with me. I presume that there will be no difficulty in our leaving?'

'No, I don't think there's any need to detain you,' said Mason, and they left the office together.

Salvatori got up from his desk and wiped his damp forehead. Going over to the bar, he picked up the Hennessy bottle and poured himself a stiff brandy. He gulped it down neat, and a little colour filtered back into his putty-like cheeks.

The woman was dead. The unknown's instructions had been carried out. There was no reason why the police should suspect that he, Salvatori, had had anything to do with it. But he was uneasy. It had been a shock. He disliked violence when it came as near as it had come that night.

Clint came softly into the office. He moved so quietly that Salvatori was unaware of his presence until he spoke.

'It was simple,' said the man. 'Easy. Just a flick of the wrist and it was over.'

'Over?' said Salvatori. 'You think that it is over, eh? With the police swarming about the place?'

'They won't be able to discover anything,' broke in Clint. 'It was dark — nobody saw me. It could have been anybody.'

'And if they should find out?' said Salvatori. 'You and me — we take the rap, eh? Will it be any good our saying that we were carrying out orders? Would they believe that someone we do not know just told us that the woman was to be killed — over the telephone — like that, eh?' He snapped his fingers. 'Would they believe that, eh?'

'It won't come to that,' said Clint.

'I am getting out,' declared Salvatori. 'I am full up. Fielding, Hyams, and now this woman ... I have finished. I do not like all this killing.'

'Do you think you'd be allowed to get out?' said Clint. 'Shall I tell you what would happen if you tried? You'd be found at the side of a lonely road, and there'd be so many bullet holes in your fat hide that they could use you as a strainer.'

'So — we go on, eh?' cried Salvatori. 'We go on taking the chances and the risks. It is foolishness. If we knew who was giving the orders — that would make it even. It is too one-sided.'

'You get paid for it, don't you?' snapped Clint.

'Will that do me any good in prison?'

'You haven't gone there yet.'

'Yet — it is the operational word,' grunted Salvatori.

Clint made no reply, but the seed had been sown. The flower of discontent was sprouting in his mind, and it was not destined to wither and die.

* ★ *

Sergeant Tickler had succeeded in weeding out most of the people in the Eldorado who had been present when the unknown knife-thrower had put an end to Vanya's life. He had taken their names and addresses and let them depart. Among these were Slade and Lydia.

On the narrow pavement outside the restaurant, Slade turned to his companion. 'I'm going to send you home in a taxi,' he said. 'I want to have a look round at the back of this place.'

Lydia was a little white under her make-up. The sudden and completely unexpected tragedy had shaken her. 'Do you think the murder of that poor woman has anything to do with this business?' she asked.

Slade frowned. 'It's difficult to tell. It may not. A murder in this district is not uncommon, you know that. On the other hand, this is a different sort of crime to the usual. It could have been connected with something in the woman's past life — a love affair. That seems to me the most likely. I don't see what motive the bunch we're after could have had.'

He hailed a passing cab. 'I'll get in touch with you in the usual way,' he said as Lydia got in. 'Sleep well, and look after yourself.'

When the cab had driven away, he walked slowly up the street. Turning at the end, he made his way round to the back of the Eldorado, and as he had more or less expected, found himself facing the shop of the masks and dummies. There was no doubt, although he couldn't actually see because of the intervening properties, that the restaurant backed onto the mask shop. There appeared to be some kind of small yard between.

He went back to the front of the restaurant. There were still several people standing about, talking on the pavement, and the glass doors were open. The vestibule was empty. Slade looked sharply right and left. Nobody was watching him — they were all too excited discussing the murder to take any notice of what he was doing — and he slipped inside the restaurant.

His object was to get through to the back of the premises and prove to himself that there was an exit that abutted onto the mask shop. At the side of the vestibule, near the desk, was a closed door. Slade opened it cautiously and found that it gave admittance to a narrow passage that was lit by a dim bulb in the roof. He stepped inside and closed the door. The passage seemed to run along the entire length of the building. It was dingy and undecorated. Probably, he thought, a service passage used only by the staff.

He explored further. The passage followed the curve of the inner wall that formed one side of the restaurant, and presently he found further progress barred by a heavy wooden door, strongly built, with diagonal braces running across it. Two bolts at the top and bottom and a large mortice lock secured it. The bolts were shot, but Slade cautiously pulled them back. There was a key in the lock and he turned it. When he pulled gently on the handle, the door opened.

A cold wind blew into the passage, and looking out, Slade saw that the door gave access to a small, oblong back yard. It was bounded on one side by the bulk of a tall building and on the other by a high wall. At the bottom was the back of another building from which an iron fire-escape ran up to the floors above. Beside the foot of this iron ladder was a closed door and a long, narrow window. According to Slade's calculations, this window and door should belong to the mask shop.

He stepped out into the yard, closing the door behind him. The place was full of empty crates and broken packing cases, several dustbins, and a great deal of other rubbish. It hadn't been tidied up or swept for months, to judge from its condition.

He picked his way carefully across to the door in the building facing him. It was a stout door that at one time had been painted green, but was now a dirty blue from the bleaching of many suns. It was locked. He peered into the window, but the glass was so grimy that he could see nothing. It offered an easier mode of ingress than the door, he thought as he took out a pocket knife.

Opening the largest blade, he inserted

it between the sashes and, after some difficulty, succeeded in pressing back the catch. The window hadn't been opened for some time, and it was all he could do to raise the lower sash sufficiently to get his fingers under it. But he managed it, and presently had got it open enough to wriggle through.

He knew that he was in the mask shop by the smell of wax before he could see anything of his surroundings — the smell of wax and the odour of papier-mâché. He pulled from his pocket a pencil-torch and sent the thin, narrow ray darting through the darkness.

He was in the work-room where he had first heard the toneless voice of the unknown. The window, which he had thought to be at the back, was the one he had noticed then. It was in the side wall and so was the door. This room then, and therefore the shop, did not *back* onto the restaurant. It was at right angles to the yard. His calculations had been wrong in that respect.

Before he began his inspection of the premises, he carefully closed the window. As he did so, he was conscious of the faint sound of dance music coming from somewhere not very far away. He remembered that he had heard it on that first occasion. It certainly didn't come from the Eldorado. There was probably a club or a café close by. In that district every other place was a club or café.

He began a close search of the workroom. After a little while he managed to find the loudspeaker from which the unknown voice had come. It was up near the dirty ceiling in one corner, and a wire ran down from it to an oblong box behind some of the half-finished masks on the shelves. The box was locked, but Slade guessed what it contained: radio receiving equipment, as he had originally suspected on his first visit. He would have liked to have made sure of this, but he had no means of opening the box except by forcing it, and that would give the fact away that someone had been there.

He was glad, however, to guess at its existence. It would be useless to arrange anything in the nature of a raid on the premises, supposing that another interview were held there. The unknown could be streets away and the raid would be abortive. Maybe the experts could fix up something that would pinpoint the place from where the man was speaking.

Slade worked his way carefully through the workshop, but he found nothing more to reward him for his diligence. The communicating door to the shop was locked, and again there was no means of opening it except by force. He concluded that it was hardly likely he would find anything of significance there in any case.

He went back to the window, opened it, and climbed into the yard. He had no intention of going back into the restaurant, and decided to try the wall and see where that led. Shutting the window, he made his way to the wall and looked up at it. It was fairly high, but there were several packing-cases nearby, and he succeeded in scrambling on top of them. By this means he was able to reach up and grip the top of the wall with his hands. He pulled himself up until he was astride, and looked down on the other side. It was a similar yard to the one at the back of the Eldorado. The dance music was a little louder here, but it didn't come from the building to which the yard belonged. That was in complete darkness.

Slade dropped into the yard and looked about him. It was cleaner than the other yard. There was a sudden clatter, and he swung round, but it was only a disturbed cat at one of the dustbins. It made off across the wall with an angry meow.

He seemed to have exchanged one dead end for another. There was neither window nor door in the wall that must form the shop part of the mask shop. It was a blank stretch of old brickwork that ran from one high wall to another, enclosing the yard on three sides. On the fourth side, the bulk of a high building reared up into the gloom of the night, silhouetted against the glow from the lights of the West End.

Slade decided to try the other wall and see where it led to. He was beginning to wish that he had gone back through the restaurant passage after all. There were no packing-cases here to help him, but he was lucky enough to find a ladder lying near the house. A few seconds later he was looking over the other wall into a narrow passage that ran between it and a similar wall on the other side. He slid down from the wall into the passage and found that a couple of yards further along it came out into the street on which the mask shop opened.

A taxi was passing and Slade hailed it. As he settled into the corner and lit a cigarette, he thought it had been quite an evening.

7

The next few days, so far as John Slade was concerned, were devoid of incident. He led his rather peculiar life, going to the Ministry of Defence every morning, slipping out the back way a few minutes later, and returning in time to leave the office by the front entrance with the rest of the staff.

So far as he could discover, he was no longer being watched. Apparently, after this first deal with the unknown, his *bona fides* had been accepted. He wasn't fool enough to take any risks, however, and he continued to behave in the character of Felton, or at least how he imagined that he would behave. He had been to the shop in Clapham and had an interview with Hallowes, and they had both agreed that a decent interval must be allowed to elapse before he made any move to sell the unknown further 'secret documents'.

At the end of the fourth day, a small packet arrived at his flat. It contained a camera of the finest workmanship and several rolls of microfilm. There was a printed folder containing full instructions on its use, but nothing else.

The unknown had been as good as his word. He had promised to send a camera and it had come.

The newspapers were full of the murder at the Eldorado, but so far there had been no arrest. The killing of Vanya was a mystery, and it looked like that was the way it was going to stay. In spite of Emile Salvatori's misgivings concerning the effect it would have on the restaurant's business, the place was more popular than ever. To its excellent food and wine had been added the thrill of dining in a place where a few nights before a woman had been stabbed to death, and the receptionist couldn't take the bookings fast enough.

Inspector Mason, at his wits' end to find a solution, paid a visit to Rodney Barney of Barney's Variety Agency. 'I'm sorry to trouble you again, sir,' he said when he was shown into the agent's office, 'but I'm hoping that you can give me some information.'

'I'll do anything I can, of course,' said

Barney. 'But I'm afraid there's very little to add to what I've already told you. Have a cigar?'

Mason shook his head. 'No, thank you, sir,' he said. 'Can you tell me anything about a man named Hyams?'

Barney raised his eyebrows. 'Hyams,' he repeated, and smiled. 'I know quite a number of people named Hyams. Which particular one are you referring to?'

'Leslie Hyams,' said the inspector. 'He was a friend of the murdered woman's. He was killed in a street accident a few weeks ago.'

Barney nodded. 'I know who you mean now,' he said. 'He was killed by a car — a hit-and-run affair. He was engaged to Vanya.'

'So I understand,' replied Mason. 'He had a police record. Did you know that?'

'I knew very little about him. Vanya didn't talk much about him to me, you see. She knew I was against it.' He took a cigarette from a box on the desk and lit it.

'Against what, sir?' asked Mason.

'The engagement,' answered the variety agent, blowing out a little cloud of smoke.

'Why was that, sir?'

'Well, you know how it is with these women. You work your guts out to build 'em up, and then they go and fall for the first good-looking fellow that comes along. A bit of running round's all right, but marriage ... it can ruin a woman's career. Why are you so interested in Hyams, eh? He couldn't have had anything to do with the murder, could he?'

Mason gave the stereotypical reply. 'Just a matter of routine, sir,' he said. 'We're interested in everyone who was connected with the dead woman.'

'Including me, I suppose?'

'Including you, sir,' agreed Mason gravely.

As he was leaving, the blonde woman who had been with the variety agent on the night of the murder at the Eldorado was shown in. 'Sit down, Peggy,' said Barney. 'I'm sorry I can't be of more help, Inspector.'

'I'm sorry, too, sir,' said Mason.

'Who was that?' asked Peggy as the inspector went out.

'That's Inspector Mason,' said Barney.

'He's in charge of the inquiry into Vanya's death.'

Peggy shivered. 'It was terrible,' she said. 'I'll never forget it. I thought I was going to faint when I saw all that blood.'

Barney made a grimace. 'You looked to me as if you were enjoying it,' he said. 'Never mind that. Look here, they want someone to take Vanya's place. I could get you forty a week.'

'Me?' cried Peggy. 'Oh, I couldn't. I should be scared to death —'

'Don't be silly,' Barney broke in impatiently. 'Lightning doesn't strike twice in the same place. I've been on to Salvatori — he's the manager — and I can fix you a contract. A month certain with an option. It's a classy place, and the work's easy.'

She looked at him doubtfully. 'I don't like the idea.'

'Look here, my dear. Work's not so easy to come by these days. Don't turn down a good opportunity because you've got some stupid idea. Come in tomorrow afternoon, and I'll have the contract ready for you to sign. Okay?'

'Well, if you think it's all right,' she said.

'Of course it's all right. Come in tomorrow.'

*   *   *

The man at the wheel of the car looked at Clint in the seat beside him. 'What was the idea?' he asked. 'Why did you suggest this tour round the side streets of London?'

'I wanted to talk to you where we couldn't be overheard,' said Clint.

Mr. Snow turned the car into another street and decreased the speed slightly. 'What's the idea?' he demanded.

'I'm not satisfied,' answered Clint. 'Not the way things are.'

'What do you mean? What's gone wrong?'

Clint shook his head. 'Nothing — it's not that,' he answered. 'It's this. The boss is making a hell of a lot of money out of this racket. The profits must be enormous.'

Mr. Snow shot him a sharp sidelong glance. 'Well?' he inquired as Clint paused. 'Go on. What's on your mind?'

'What are we getting?' said Clint. 'A small cut, that's all, and we take all the risks. It's not good enough — it's too one-sided.'

'I agree with you so far,' said Mr. Snow. 'What do you suggest we do about it? Resign?'

'Don't be stupid. I'm serious,' snapped Clint. 'If we knew who it was we were working for, it would even things up a bit, wouldn't it?'

'Would it?' said Mr. Snow. He swung the car round another corner.

'We'd be in a position to bargain, wouldn't we?'

Mr. Snow pursed his rather thick lips. 'Hyams thought that,' he remarked.

'Hyams was a fool!' declared Clint impatiently.

'You're suggesting that we do the same thing.'

'I'm suggesting that we find out who's running this outfit, but I'm not suggesting we use the knowledge in the stupid way that Hyams did.' He took out a packet of Gold Flakes and lit one.

'Does Salvatori think the same?' asked Mr. Snow. 'Is he in on this?'

Clint shook his head. 'No,' he replied, trickling smoke through his nostrils 'I don't trust him. He's yellow. Are you with me?'

The other considered for a moment before he answered. 'I suppose you realize just how dangerous it's going to be?'

'You don't have to take any risks,' interposed Clint. 'All I want you to do is this. You always know when there's a deal coming off, don't you? It's your job to meet the seller and take him to the shop. Well, next time you do it, tip me off. I'll do the rest.'

'I see. You want to know the time and the date, eh? Well, that shouldn't be difficult. But what good's it going to do you? You won't be any nearer finding out who's running the outfit.'

'You leave that to me,' said Clint.

'All right, it's a deal.'

'Remember — this is between us,' warned Clint. 'Don't talk!'

The other gave a harsh laugh without hint of mirth. 'Don't worry, I'm not such a fool,' he retorted. 'I don't want to get my throat cut one dark night. What are you going to do,' he added curiously, 'when you do find out?'

'I'm going to see that we get our fair share,' replied Clint. 'More than the pittance we get now.'

'It's not exactly a pittance.'

'It is, in comparison.'

'Well, I hope you're lucky. Now, I think you'd better get out.' He drew into the kerb and pulled up.

'What are you scared about?' asked Clint.

Mr. Snow shrugged his shoulders. 'I'm fond of living. If you like to commit suicide, that's your business. But I'd rather not be with you when you do it.'

Clint got out. 'You're as bad as Salvatori,' he sneered.

Mr. Snow made no reply. Almost before his passenger had reached the pavement, he drove away.

*   *   *

It was at the expiration of ten days when Slade decided that sufficient time had been allowed to elapse before he contacted the unknown head of the organization with reference to a fresh deal. Accordingly, there appeared in the board outside the newsagent's shop in Greek Street a card bearing the following advertisement:

For Sale. Navy overcoat. Suit medium-sized man. Bargain. £4 10d. Inquire within.

He left his name and address with the shopkeeper as before, and awaited developments.

They were not long in coming. The following morning there was a letter in the wire basket behind the front door of his flat. It had been delivered by hand and was short and to the point:

Be at the shop with the masks tonight at eleven.

Slade had already provided himself with the microfilm of a supposed new submarine base situated off the coast of Ireland. It wasn't such good value, perhaps, as the previous 'secrets' he had supplied, but he thought it would be sufficient to interest the unknown.

As soon as he had paid his usual visit to the office and escaped by the back way, he took a bus to Clapham Junction and sought out Hallowes. Weldon was rearranging the stock on his counter when Slade entered and, as the shop was empty, greeted him with a beaming smile. 'The super's in the back room,' he said. 'How's life, Mr. Slade?'

'Very precarious,' answered Slade.

Weldon made a grimace. 'You know, I often wish I was back at the old game. Retiring is all right for a bit, but you get that you'd like a bit of the old excitement.'

'You can have all mine,' said Slade, and he went in search of Hallowes.

'Eleven o'clock tonight, is it?' said the superintendent, when he heard what Slade had to tell him. 'Hm. Well, how are you going to play it, eh? Want any help yet?'

'Yes — Lydia,' answered Slade promptly. 'I want her to meet me for dinner at the Eldorado. Tell her to get herself up like she did before. I'll meet her there at eight.'

'And then?' inquired Hallowes.

'Can you arrange for a Q-Squad van to patrol in the vicinity of the mask shop? I want it fitted with a direction-finding radio instrument.'

'That's all ready for you,' interrupted the superintendent smoothly. 'When you told me about that box an' what you believed it might contain, I rather guessed you'd want something of the sort when you'd fixed another interview. Why Lydia?'

'I'd like to have someone in the yard at the back of the restaurant. No, no, I'm not suggesting that Lydia should be the one.'

'I should hope not,' grunted Hallowes. 'I'll see that there's someone there, but what do you want Lydia for?'

'I want her to try and have a look round the premises of the Eldorado — the private part,' explained Slade. 'It'll be better for a woman to do that. There's less likelihood of her being suspected if anyone sees her. She can always shoot a line that she's lost her way looking for the ladies' room.'

'You think she might spot that fellow she followed?' said Hallowes. 'Is that the idea?'

'Yes,' answered Slade. 'Then we'll be certain that the Eldorado is mixed up in this business. At present it's pure speculation.'

'I'll arrange for one of our operatives to be in that yard,' said the superintendent, 'and the Q-car. Now, is there anything else?'

Slade shook his head. 'I can't think of anything at the moment. It's going to be a difficult job catching the King Pippin.'

'I never expected that it 'ud be easy,' grunted Hallowes. 'We've got to be careful that he doesn't slip through our fingers.'

When Slade had gone, Hallowes sat smoking thoughtfully for a minute or two, then he pulled the phone towards him and dialled a number. 'Hallowes here,' he said. 'I've a job for you, Rudge. There's a place called the Eldorado — oh you know it, eh? Well, it backs onto a shop that sells dummies and masks. There's a small yard between the two buildings.' He explained the layout carefully. 'I want you to be in that yard at about half-past ten tonight. You'd better make yourself look like a loafer, in case you're caught.'

'What do I do when I get there?' asked Rudge.

'Use your intelligence,' grunted the superintendent. 'Keep your eyes open and watch everything that goes on. I don't want you to take any action, whatever you see — just note it. Understand?'

Detective-Inspector Rudge, who was also attached to that band of unknown operatives called the Ghost Squad, said that he understood, and Hallowes rang off.

A few seconds later he was talking to the superintendent in charge of E Division. 'I want that Q-car I talked to you about to patrol the vicinity of the Eldorado tonight,' he said when he had revealed who he was. 'It can start about ten o'clock. I want to know the location of any radio that you can pick up. It will probably be on a wavelength similar to the car's two-way radio. See if you can spot it.'

When this had been attended to, he rang up Lydia and made arrangements for her to meet Slade at the Eldorado. 'He'll tell you what he wants you to do,' he concluded. 'And be careful. Don't forget that you're dealing with a dangerous bunch.'

He lay back in his chair and slowly refilled his pipe. There was nothing more he could do except await the reports from the people he had set in motion, like a puppet-master controlling his figures. Only there were other figures — unknown figures — that he could not control.

★ ★ ★

It was a cold night with a clear sky from which the stars glittered with a frosty brilliance. Even the glare of the West End advertisement signs could not entirely dim their brightness.

The Q-car travelled slowly the length of Frith Street, negotiated the roundabout at Cambridge Circus, and ran along Shaftesbury Avenue. It was a very ordinary-looking delivery van with the name and address of a grocery store painted in dingy lettering on the equally dingy sides. Both the name and address were fictitious. Inside, Inspector Arnold Lake and a wireless operator waited expectantly by the radio detector that took up most of the available room.

'Anything?' asked Lake.

'No, sir,' answered the operator.

Lake grunted and lighted a cigarette. He could see out the gauze-covered aperture in one of the sides that was invisible from the outside. They had turned into Windmill Street and were preparing to negotiate the maze of side streets that lay at the back of the avenue.

He was interested in this assignment, but would have liked to know more about it. The chief divisional superintendent had given him his instructions, but had omitted to explain what it was all about. He had to find the exact spot from which a two-way radio might be operated that night. But who would be operating it, and what lay behind it, was something that Lake had not been told. Why the unusual secrecy? As a rule, he was thoroughly well-briefed. But tonight the information given him had been meagre, to say the least.

He looked at his watch. It was getting on for twenty to eleven and, so far, nothing had happened, or they had failed to pick it up. The wireless operator was twiddling his controls, trying various wavelengths, but up to now without result. Lake wondered how long they were supposed to do this 'round and round the mulberry bush' business. Until headquarters came through with the order to stop, he supposed.

The streets were becoming crowded as the theatres and cinemas broke and their audiences made their way to their respective homes. It didn't usually last long, this crowded period; and then the streets would gradually become less and less congested until they were given up to patrolling policemen and those denizens of the night who seldom appeared in the light of day.

The Q-car continued its monotonous patrol.

*　*　*

Detective-Inspector Rudge dropped lightly down from the top of the wall into the yard behind the Eldorado. It was a little after half-past ten; and at that particular moment, although Rudge didn't know it, Inspector Lake was in the Q-car, passing the entrance to the restaurant. Neither Rudge nor Lake were aware that inside the Eldorado, John Slade and Lydia were just finishing their meal.

'If I come here many more times,' remarked the latter as she accepted a cigarette from her companion's case, and dipped the end into the flame of the lighter he held out to her, 'I shall have to go on a strict diet. All this food is going to play havoc with my figure.'

'It's going to do the same to the expense account figure,' said Slade, glancing at the bill that lay beside his plate. 'You'd better be thinking of powdering your nose in a minute,' he continued. 'I'll pay this and slip out while you've gone. Try and see if you can dodge into the private part of the building. There's probably a door somewhere that leads —'

'Off the vestibule,' she interrupted calmly. 'I saw it as we came in.' She rose gracefully to her feet. 'I'll meet you in the front,' she said loudly for the benefit of the waiters, and walked slowly through the nearly empty restaurant.

Slade watched her go with slight misgivings. He had never got used to working with a woman on these dangerous missions. It seemed all wrong, somehow, that she should be exposed to the peril that was part and parcel of an operative's job. But she had chosen the job herself, as Hallowes had once pointed out.

He called the waiter and paid the bill, walked out to the cloakroom, and collected his hat and coat. There was no sign of Lydia, but he saw the door she had mentioned and concluded that she was exploring the private portion beyond.

There was nobody in the vestibule, and he went out into the street. An approaching taxi slowed down hopefully, but he ignored it. As he turned into the street where the mask shop was situated, a van passed him slowly, but Slade scarcely glanced at it. He had no means of knowing that it was the Q-car which he had asked Hallowes to arrange to patrol the district. He paused outside the mask shop and looked in the window. Looking quickly up and down the street, he went to the door and grasped the handle. It opened under his hand and he slipped inside.

Closing the door quickly behind him, he looked at his watch. It was five minutes to eleven. The door to the work-room was unlocked this time, and he went in. It was very dim here. The only light came through the dirty window in the side wall.

He looked at his watch. It was nearly eleven. Any moment now, that weird voice would break the silence of that room from the concealed speaker.

Even as the thought drained out of his mind, it did: 'Are you there, Felton?'

Although Slade had been expecting it, the sudden sound of that hollow voice coming out of nowhere made his heart jump. 'Yes, I'm here,' he answered.

114

'What have you got?' inquired the voice.

'The plans for a new submarine base off the coast of Ireland,' he replied. 'I have the microfilms.'

'That is not a very important thing,' said the voice. 'Have you brought the films with you?'

'No,' said Slade. 'I concluded that you would pick them up like you did last time.'

'They will not be worth much. Perhaps a couple of hundred.'

'I'll have something better soon,' said Slade. 'I thought this information might be useful —'

'I'll buy it,' broke in the voice. 'You will get your instructions tomorrow.'

'Can't we dispense with all this nonsense?' asked Slade impatiently. 'Why can't we just meet somewhere?'

'Because I prefer my own methods,' said the voice curtly. 'There is something that I would be willing to pay a very good price for, if you could get it.'

'What's that?'

'The defence plans in the event of a nuclear attack.'

'That would be difficult to get.'

'But you could get them?'

'I suppose I could. But the risk would be pretty great. I should have to be careful.'

'Five thousand pounds is worth being careful for,' said the voice.

'It would take time.'

'How long?'

'I can't tell exactly. I should have to wait for the right opportunity.'

'When you have the information, let me know in the usual way.'

'For that kind of information,' said Slade, 'five thousand isn't much.'

'Providing the information is complete, I would be prepared to pay more. We can discuss that when you have obtained it. You will be hearing from me.'

There was a click. The unknown had gone.

The Q-car, drawn up in a side street, began to move slowly again. The radio expert had succeeded in picking up the latter part of the conversation between Slade and the unknown. 'It's coming from somewhere quite close, sir,' he informed Lake. 'Try going up this next turning.'

The inspector gave instructions to the driver. They turned the corner and moved slowly along the street. The man at the direction-finder fiddled with a series of knobs. 'It's stronger now,' he said. 'Keep going in this direction.'

The Q-car ran slowly past the mask shop and on to the end of the street. 'It's somewhere quite close here,' said the radio expert. 'Turn right.'

The driver obeyed the instructions.

'Keep going,' muttered the radio expert, his fingers moving quickly over the instrument panel. 'I'll have it in a minute ... ' He broke off with an exclamation.

'What's the matter?' asked Inspector Lake.

'He's switched off,' answered the other disgustedly. 'Just as I was getting warm.' He turned a knob slowly. 'Pull up, will you?'

The car came to a halt at the kerb, and they waited. At the expiration of twenty minutes, the radio expert took off his headphones and shook his head. 'No good,' he announced. 'He's shut down.'

★ ★ ★

117

Detective-Inspector Rudge, lurking in the shelter of a pile of packing-cases, came to the conclusion that he was wasting his time. Except for a stray cat that had stopped and stared at him curiously, there had been no sign of life in the yard at the back of the Eldorado. Rudge had been instructed to watch for anyone who might come into the yard, but nobody had. He wondered what it was all about. Like Inspector Lake, his instructions had not carried with them any explanation. He was just supposed to keep watch and note down what he saw.

Well, he had seen nothing except the cat. Was he supposed to put *that* in his report? If he didn't, it would be a blank sheet of paper.

It was very cold, and he shivered. How much longer was it worth staying here? he wondered.

★　★　★

Lydia walked slowly along a thickly carpeted corridor. Beyond the door in the vestibule, she had discovered a flight of stairs that had brought her to a small landing from which the corridor ran left and right. She had chosen the right-hand arm.

This was the private part of the restaurant. There were two closed doors in one wall, and the other wall was blank. It was completely silent here. She came to the end of the passage and was confronted by a curtained window. She looked about for a second, and decided to try the other arm of the corridor.

Noiselessly, she made her way back to the landing. This arm was shorter than the other. There was a curtained window at the end of this, too, but only one door broke the stretch of wall. She paused outside and listened, but there was no sound from within.

Suddenly Lydia heard the door at the bottom of the stairs open. Somebody was coming up! She moved quickly to the window at the end of the corridor and slipped behind the heavy curtains. A man appeared from the direction of the landing and came along the passage. It was the manager of the restaurant, Salvatori! He stopped at the closed door, turned the handle and went in.

Lydia let her breath escape slowly. So far she had discovered nothing of any importance. It was only natural that Salvatori should be there. The room he had entered was probably an office or a private apartment — she supposed that he lived on the premises.

She wondered what she ought to do. Her exploration of the private part of the Eldorado hadn't been very successful, but she couldn't very well remain much longer. If she were discovered, the explanation that she was looking for the ladies' room would sound a bit dubious. Somebody would remember how long it had been since she'd left the restaurant. It was scarcely likely that she would have been searching all that time.

She came out from behind the curtain and moved silently towards the landing. As she reached it, a man who had come soundlessly up the stairs suddenly confronted her. 'What are you doing here?' he demanded suspiciously.

It was the man she had followed from the tea-shop.

8

'What are you doing here?' asked Clint again. 'This is private. You've no right up here.'

'I was looking for the ladies' room,' said Lydia.

'It's downstairs — on the other side of the vestibule,' answered Clint, his small eyes like chips of flint. 'This door is plainly marked 'private'.'

'There's no need to be rude,' retorted Lydia. 'I made a mistake. I'm sorry.'

'I've seen you before somewhere,' he said, still barring her way to the staircase.

'No doubt you have,' she said. 'I was dining here. If you are connected with the restaurant —'

'That's right,' he broke in quickly. 'You were with Felton.'

'I was with *Mr.* Felton, yes,' she answered, stressing the 'Mr.' 'Please let me pass. He will be wondering what has happened to me.'

'He's gone,' said Clint.

'Gone?' Her expression of surprise was perfect. 'He wouldn't go without me.'

'Well, he's not downstairs.'

'Perhaps he thinks I've gone and is looking for me outside,' she said. 'Really, I think you are behaving in a most extraordinary manner.'

'What is the matter? Who is this lady?' broke in the voice of Salvatori. He had come out of his office and was standing behind them.

Lydia turned quickly. 'You are the manager, aren't you?' she said.

Salvatori bowed. 'Yes, madam,' he answered. 'I can do something for you, yes?'

'You can tell this man to let me pass,' she said angrily. 'I don't know who he is, but he's been extremely offensive.'

'This woman was prowling about up here,' put in Clint. 'I found her. She was with Felton in the restaurant.' Salvatori frowned.

'I have explained that I was looking for the ladies' room,' said Lydia. 'I am not accustomed to this kind of treatment.'

'No, no, of course, of course,' said

Salvatori with a glare at Clint. 'I am very sorry — please accept my apology, madam.'

'I shall certainly speak to Mr. Felton,' she said.

'Do,' interrupted Clint with a sneer.

'Be silent!' Salvatori turned on him like a tiger. 'You will apologize at once on the instant to this lady. You hear?'

'All right, I'm sorry,' muttered Clint sullenly.

'There — I am sure that you are satisfied, madam,' said Salvatori, his fat face wreathed in smiles. 'It was unfortunate. I myself will escort you to the vestibule.'

He led the way down the stairs. Clint stood for a moment watching them, then he turned away and went into the office.

'Where is Mr. Felton?' asked Salvatori when they reached the vestibule. ''E is not 'ere.'

'Perhaps he thought I'd gone,' said Lydia. She flashed him a dazzling smile. 'It seems to have been an unfortunate ending to a very pleasant evening.'

'I am sorry,' said Salvatori. 'You would like to wait, yes — in case Mr. Felton should return?'

She shook her head. 'I'll get a taxi, I think,' she said. 'I'm rather tired.'

'Allow me to arrange it,' said the manager eagerly.

He went quickly to the door and looked up and down the street. A taxi was crawling along on the other side of the road and he hailed it vigorously. When it drew in to the kerb, he insisted on escorting Lydia across the pavement. She gave the driver her address and got in. Salvatori shut the door, and she saw him standing, a resplendent figure, looking after the cab as it drove away.

She had not discovered much, but her efforts had not been entirely wasted. She had definitely established a connection between the Eldorado and the people working for the unknown man whom they were trying to find. That man with the hard eyes and thin mouth had something to hide; his attitude had shown that. And she was not very impressed with Salvatori. There was an oiliness about him that she disliked.

Slade would be interested. She wondered how he had got on at the interview.

*　*　*

Slade reached his flat just before midnight. He was glad to get back. The night was very cold, and the room was warm and comfortable after the draughty shop and his journey. He had left the electric fire burning before he went out.

He went into his bedroom and returned a few seconds later in dressing-gown and slippers. He believed in comfort — when he had the chance. You never knew in this precarious job what sort of character you were going to be next. You might be living in some vermin-infested room in a slum.

He poured himself out a large Haig, squirted in a small portion of soda, and carried the drink over to the fire.

He wondered how the Q-car had fared. Had they succeeded in tracing the spot from which the unknown had spoken? And had Lydia found out anything? He was a little worried about her. These people wouldn't be squeamish if they thought someone was spying on them. But she was experienced; one of their best operatives. She knew how to take care of herself. There was Rudge, too. That had been a long shot. The unknown might have altered his usual arrangements and instead of using the radio come himself to the mask shop. It was an unlikely contingency, but one that had to be allowed for. He would hear what had happened from Hallowes in the morning.

Slade sighed. He was tired, and he felt that he would be glad when this job was over. This masquerading in someone else's personality was very wearing. That was the worst part of this job. You never had any time to be yourself. He wondered what character he would be called on to impersonate next. A spiv living in a back room in Soho, probably.

He finished the whisky, yawned, and got wearily to his feet. Bed was the best thing. It didn't matter whether he was Felton, Slade, or a dead cat when he was asleep. He was halfway to the door when the front door bell rang.

He stopped, frowning. Who could it be at this hour? It wouldn't be Lydia or Hallowes. They wouldn't come to the flat in case it should be watched. It must be one of the group.

The bell rang again, a long shrill summons that reflected the impatience of the person who rang. Slade went out into the hall and opened the door.

'What the blazes do you want at this hour?' he began angrily.

'All right, let me come in,' broke in a man's voice urgently. I want to talk to you.'

Without waiting for permission, he forced his way into the hall. Slade recognized him instantly. It was one of the men who had been watching the flat — the one who had followed him to the tea-shop.

'Look here, I don't know who you are,' he protested in pretended ignorance, 'but if you don't get out of here —'

'It's all right, Felton,' said Clint. I'm part of the set-up.'

'What set-up?' demanded Slade. 'I don't know what the hell you're talking about.'

'I'm talking about the mask shop,' said Clint. 'Now do you understand?'

Be careful, thought Slade. *This may be a trick. It's just the sort of thing they'd try.* 'You must be mad, or else you've come to the wrong address,' he said. 'I don't know anything about a mask shop.'

127

'Listen,' said Clint. 'I'll tell you what you've been doing there — everything you've done during the past few weeks. Will that convince you?'

Without waiting for a reply, he began. When he had finished, he said: 'Well, does that satisfy you that I'm in this business?'

'What do you want?' asked Slade. 'Have you brought me a message?'

Clint shook his head. 'No,' he answered. 'I'm here on my own account. I don't mind telling you, Felton, that I'm not satisfied. The whole business is too one-sided.'

'I haven't the least idea what you're talking about. But you'd better come in for a moment,' said Slade. He led the way into the lounge. Pouring out two Haigs, he gave one to Clint. 'Now,' he demanded, 'what's this all about?'

Clint told him, and Slade listened with mixed emotions. Surprise was mingled with elation. This might be a situation that could be used to his advantage. A rift in the smooth running of the unknown's organization could only result in the eventual fall of the whole structure. Slade decided that Clint's dissatisfaction must be encouraged.

'You must have been a pretty trusting lot to put up with the arrangement,' he remarked when Clint had finished. 'This fellow could double-cross you any time he wanted to, and you couldn't do anything about it.'

'The money is good,' said Clint, 'but it's not enough. He's getting the lion's share, and we do all the work and take all the risks.'

'Well, what do you propose to do about it?'

'You've got a deal coming off with him. You will be meeting him soon to complete it. I want to know where the appointment is.'

Slade pretended to be dubious. 'I don't know whether I can do that,' he said. 'It might spoil things for me.'

'Nobody will know except me. The meeting will be on some stretch of country road; it always is. All I want you to do is to tell me what time and where.'

'You're going to try and follow this fellow and find out who he is?' Clint nodded. 'Then what?'

The other shrugged his thin shoulders. 'It'll make things more even. Maybe I could get a better deal for myself.'

'Blackmail?' suggested Slade bluntly.

'I prefer to call it a bargaining angle.'

Slade considered. 'How do I know this isn't a trick to test me out?' he said after a pause.

'You don't,' answered Clint. 'You'll have to take my word that it isn't.'

'It's a risk.'

'It cuts both ways. You could tell the big fellow what I've said, couldn't you? He has a pretty drastic way of dealing with people who try to find out his identity.'

Slade remembered the fate of Fielding. 'I don't want to get myself mixed up in any trouble,' he said. 'This business suits me. I need money — I like to live comfortably. This way I get quick money for very little risk. I don't want to do anything that will put a stop to that.'

'Listen,' said Clint, leaning forward. 'I've a proposition to make to you.'

'Well, make it quickly,' broke in Slade with a yawn. 'I'm tired. I've got to be at the office by nine-thirty, and late nights don't agree with me.'

'It's simple. I'll buy anything you've got

to sell — if it's good.'

'I see.' Slade nodded. 'You're going into the business on your own account, eh?'

'You can put it like that.'

'What I've got is worth money in the right quarter. Therefore it *costs* money.'

'I can find the money,' said Clint. 'Is it a deal?'

Slade frowned. 'I'll have to think about it. Give me a ring at eight o'clock tomorrow morning — or rather, it's this morning now. I'll give you my answer then.'

'Whatever it is, you'll keep this visit of mine to yourself?' said Clint. 'I don't want to figure as the corpse in a murder case.'

Slade promised, and the man took his departure. When he had gone, Slade went back to the lounge, poured himself out another Haig, lighted a cigarette, and pondered over what had just happened. It was something that he might have expected. In his experience, he had found it continuously happening. Sooner or later, even in the best-run organization, there would be a weak link. He thought that Clint might be very useful. Why shouldn't *he* do the dangerous work of finding out the unknown's identity? If there was any slip, Clint would get the kicks.

When he finally went to bed, Slade had decided to agree.

* * *

At ten o'clock the following morning, the little room at the back of Weldon's shop contained three people. Hallowes sat in his usual chair, smoking his inevitable pipe. Facing him were Slade and Lydia.

'I think it was a wise move to agree,' said Hallowes when he heard what Clint had proposed. 'It could very well save us a lot of time and trouble. If this man finds out who the kingpin of the outfit is, it shouldn't be difficult for us to find out through him.'

'He's the man I ran into in the Eldorado last night,' put in Lydia. 'A really nasty piece of work. I should think he would be capable of anything.'

'Entirely ruthless,' said Slade.

'I'm sorry I didn't get a chance to find out more,' said Lydia.

'You did very well,' commented Hallowes. 'We do know that there is a connection between the Eldorado and this bunch.'

'What about Rudge?' asked Slade. 'Did he see anything?'

Hallowes shook his head. 'Nothing at all,' he declared. 'Nor did Lake in the Q-car. They were just getting on to the direction when our friend closed down. He was talking from somewhere quite close to the mask shop, though; we established that much.'

'I shall probably get my orders later,' said Slade. 'What are you going to do? Have a patrol car waiting to follow Clint?'

Hallowes knocked the ashes out of his pipe. 'No,' he answered. 'Not this time. This man we're up against is no fool. He knows that the one risky moment for him is when the exchange of money and information is made. He's taken the utmost precaution to ensure that the risk is a minimum one, but he won't relax his vigilance for a second. That's where poor Fielding went wrong. He was too quick. This fish requires playing very carefully or he'll be off the hook before we can reel him in. Let Clint do his stuff. If anything goes wrong, you'll be in the clear; and if you play your cards well, there'll be other opportunities. You seem to have established yourself as a good source of revenue. Continue to offer to supply information, and when his suspicions are completely lulled, we'll pounce.'

'He wants a complete plan of the operation to be put into force in the event of a nuclear attack,' said Slade. 'I've promised to get it for him.'

Hallowes paused in the act of refilling his pipe and whistled. 'He doesn't want much,' he remarked. 'That's going to take some doing to make it look authentic without giving anything away.'

Slade grinned. 'That's your headache. I said it'd take a little while to collect.'

'I'll get it attended to,' promised Hallowes. 'We've got another angle to this, you know — the contacts through which this fellow sells his information. We could do with some information concerning them.'

'That's the job of Special Branch,' said Slade.

'They've asked us to help. They seem to think you might have a good chance of digging up something.'

'Oh they do, do they? Don't you think I've enough on my plate without a second helping?'

'I'm not suggesting that you should make a meal of it. But if you *did* happen to come across any useful information in that line, they'd be pleased to have it.'

'I'm sure they would,' said Slade.

'What have you got for me?' asked Lydia. 'Do I continue to be taken out to dinner as Mr. Felton's girlfriend?'

'At the moment you don't even do that,' said Hallowes. 'You can take a rest for a bit.'

Lydia made a grimace. 'I shall get thin,' she said.

'You're never satisfied,' remarked Slade. 'Last night you were grumbling that you'd be getting too fat.' She laughed.

'There'll be a job for you soon,' said Hallowes.

'Meanwhile, I pay for my own meals?' she said. 'Oh well, I suppose everything has to come to an end.'

'I'll buy you a coffee,' said Slade. 'And it won't be on an expense account.'

'It had better not be,' said Hallowes.

Slade found a note when he got back to his flat that evening. It had been delivered by hand and was short and to the point.

Be at the second milestone on the Guildford Road at eleven o'clock tomorrow night.

There was no signature, but Slade knew who had sent it. He had scarcely finished reading the note when the telephone rang. He guessed that it was Clint before he heard his voice come over the wire. When he'd agreed that morning to inform Clint of the place and time of the appointment, Clint had said that he would ring. Slade read the note to him over the phone.

'All right,' said Clint. 'Now just carry on as usual. I'll do the rest.'

'Be careful,' warned Slade. 'If he sees anyone about, he'll think it's me. I don't want a bullet through the head.'

'Don't worry. You won't see any sign of me, but I'll be there.' He rang off.

Slade decided to have an early night to make up for his lack of sleep on the previous one. After paying his usual visit to the office the following morning, he spent the rest of the day in his flat, lounging about and reading, until it was time to pay his second visit to the office, and leave by the front entrance with the rest of the staff. He had dinner at a quiet little Italian restaurant in Kensington and then set off to keep his appointment.

It was a fine, cold night with a clear, star-encrusted sky. Slade reached the Guildford road just as his watch told him that it was half-past ten. He had no idea where the second milestone might be, and discovered that he was in for a long walk. He found it eventually, near a closed gate that led into a ploughed field. The milestone was partially concealed in a ditch at the side of the deserted road, and unless Slade had been especially looking for it, could easily have been missed.

He took up his position by the gate and lighted a cigarette. There was a fairly heavy frost, and he was glad he had taken the precaution of putting on a heavy sweater under his jacket. Even with this, and his overcoat, it was bitterly cold.

He could see nothing of Clint, though

he kept a sharp lookout. The road at this point was lined on either side with high, straggling hedges, and there was plenty of concealment. Clint could have taken up his position in any one of a dozen strategic places. But how did he propose to follow the unknown? He certainly couldn't expect to keep up with a car on foot. What was his plan? A motorcycle, decided Slade. That was the most likely means. But he'd have to be very cautious.

The lights of a car appeared in the distance, drew nearer, and passed by. This was followed after an interval by a heavy lorry, and then another car.

Slade looked at his watch. It was nearly eleven. The unknown should be along at any moment. The road was completely deserted now. Slade clapped his hands and stamped his feet to try and get some warmth back into them. He thought of the cosy lounge of his flat and the bottle of Haig on the sideboard. He could have done with a good stiff whisky at that moment.

Along at the end of the dark stretch of road, two pinpoints of light appeared. They got larger as the car sped nearer. *This must be it,* thought Slade. It was. The car, a different make to the one he had come in before, slowed, drew in to the kerb, and stopped.

Slade moved from the gate and onto the path. The window of the car was lowered as he came level with it, and he could dimly make out the shadowy figure in the driving-seat.

'Is that you, Felton?' asked a muffled voice.

'Yes.' Slade went closer to the open window. He brought his hand out of his pocket with a little packet. 'Here you are.'

A gloved hand was stretched through the window and the fingers closed on the packet. It was withdrawn into the car, and a moment later the hand was thrust out again with a thin packet of notes. 'There is the money,' said the muffled voice. 'Are you doing what I asked about the other business?'

'Yes,' said Slade, putting the notes into his pocket. 'I'll let you know when I have what you want.'

'In the usual way,' said the voice. The car moved forward, gathered speed quickly, and the red tail-lights began to grow smaller as it receded in the distance.

Slade waited. If Clint had been watching, he must make a move or he would lose his quarry. Ah, there he was! The sound of an engine starting reached his ears. He saw a dim light move out of the shelter of the hedge on the other side of the road and go swiftly away in the direction of the unknown's car. The motorcycle — for there was no doubt that that was what it was — must have been equipped with a powerful silencer, because there was scarcely more than a deep hum from the engine.

Slade turned away. Well, that was that! He started to walk back along the road. It was all very well for the man in the car, he thought a little irritably, but it was not very pleasant having to walk a mile or two out in the country on a freezing night.

He sighed. It was, he supposed, all part of the job.

9

Late the following afternoon, in the offices of Barney's Variety Agency, Mr. Rodney Barney was sitting at his big desk talking to Peggy, who had just sauntered languidly into the office.

'It's all fixed, my dear,' he said genially. 'You open next Monday.'

'Do you really think I ought to take it?' she inquired doubtfully. 'I've been thinking, and I don't fancy it — not one little bit, I don't.'

'How foolish can you get?' he demanded. 'This is a good chance for you. You'll be seen. All the managers come to the Eldorado.'

'That's all very well, but I can't help remembering what happened to Vanya. I'd rather stay alive and be unknown.'

'But, my dear woman, I thought we'd been into all that?' Barney said impatiently. 'There's no reason why you should be in any danger. They don't make a habit of

141

murdering their singers, you know.'

Peggy did not see any humour in the situation. 'I don't like the idea,' she said obstinately. 'Surely you can find me something else.'

'Not as good as this. Now look here, Peggy — don't be silly. This is a good chance, and good chances don't come along every day.'

Peggy frowned. With one hand on her hip in a pose she had practised before a mirror and thought was effective, she looked at Barney, pouting slightly. 'Well, if you insist,' she said reluctantly.

'Good,' he said. From a drawer in the desk he produced a contract. 'Just sign here.' She came nearer to the desk and took the pen he held out. 'On this line — here?' she asked.

He nodded, and she scrawled her signature. 'You open next Monday,' he said. 'You can rehearse from ten until eleven-thirty every morning with the pianist.'

'What about dresses?' she asked quickly.

'You find your own, dear. Here, take this to Revlon's.' He wrote quickly on a sheet of paper and gave it to her. 'They'll fix you up with a couple of evening gowns. I'll stop the cost out of your salary at the rate of five pounds a week.'

'Five pounds,' she echoed. 'That's a lot.'

'The dresses will be your property,' he said. 'You must have something really striking.'

'All right,' she agreed a little sullenly. 'But it's a lot of money.'

'It ought to be worth the outlay,' he said. 'We ought to land you a really first-class contract from this.'

'I hope you're right.'

'I'm sure of it.' He smiled. 'You're quite a good artiste, Peggy. Now, run along; I've got somebody waiting.'

She went over to the door. 'Bye,' she said.

Barney pressed down the switch of the intercom on his desk as she went out. 'Is Mr. Delmar there, May?' he asked. 'Right — send him in, will you?'

He took a cigarette from the box on the desk and lighted it. The door opened and a man came in. He was tall and dark, with a small beard and moustache that gave him a foreign appearance. He looked rather like the accepted idea of Mephistopheles — an appearance which he took a great deal of trouble to cultivate.

'Lock the door, Delmar,' said Barney.

Delmar turned the key and came over to the desk, moving with the smooth sleekness of a panther.

'Sit down,' said Barney, indicating the easy chair facing him. 'Have you brought the money?'

Delmar touched a bulky briefcase which he carried. 'It is here,' he replied with the hint of an accent. 'You ask a lot, my friend.'

'Not more than it's worth.' Barney took a key from his pocket, got up, and went over to a small safe. He unlocked it and took out a steel box. This he carried back to the desk, and with another key unlocked it. From it he produced a document. 'Here you are,' he said. 'Complete details of the new rocket sites in Great Britain. It's worth five thousand, isn't it?'

Delmar stretched out his hand. 'Let me see it,' he replied briefly.

Barney smiled and shook his head. 'Money first.'

Delmar shrugged his shoulders. 'You are cautious, my friend.'

'In these transactions, I have to be.'

Delmar opened the briefcase. From it he took out several packets of notes, which he placed carefully on the desk. 'There you are,' he said. 'Five thousand pounds.'

Barney handed him the document he had bought from Felton. While the other was examining it, he collected the money, counted it, and put it away in a drawer of the desk.

'This appears to be satisfactory,' said Delmar. He folded the document and put it in the briefcase.

'Have I ever sold you anything that wasn't?' asked Barney.

'It would go badly with you, if you did. I'm afraid you would not get a second chance, my friend. What about the other matter?'

'It is being arranged. It will cost you a lot of money. You are prepared for that?'

'If it is what I have asked for, we shall not haggle about the price, my friend. When can you obtain it?'

'It will take a little time,' replied Barney. 'I will drop in and see you during the show when I have news. It's time you introduced some new tricks into your act. A lot of it is getting out of date.'

'I am putting on a new vanishing trick next week,' said Delmar, who was billed as The Great Delmar, Prince of Magicians. 'It is good.'

'One of these days you'll be doing a vanishing act back to your own country, I expect,' remarked Barney.

'Perhaps,' answered the other. 'You may have to do a vanishing act too, my friend, but it will not be back to your own country, eh?'

'Everything comes to an end,' said Barney. 'I have taken precautions. Not even the people who work for me know who I really am.'

'You must have made a lot of money,' said Delmar. 'I am not the only person who pays you for information, eh, my friend?'

'No, but my expenses are heavy,' said Barney. He went over and put the steel box back in the safe. 'I'm arranging a new contract for you. I shall have the details in a day or so.'

Delmar got up with a sinuous movement that had something reptilian about it. 'It is a good, what do you call it? — blind, this conjuring business,' he said. 'It covers a multitude of sins, eh, my friend? Just as this business of yours does.'

'It started as a legitimate agency,' said Barney. 'It still makes a fairly good profit.'

'But not as good as the other business,' said Delmar, with a smile curving his thin lips. 'It is funny, my friend, that we should both be in the same boat, eh? I started as a legitimate conjuror, but my other business brings me more money.' He went over to the door and gently turned the key. 'I must be going. Don't forget to come and see me at the theatre — and come soon, my friend.' He slid round the partially open door and closed it softly behind him.

Barney went back to the desk. He took a cigarette from the box in front of him, looked at it thoughtfully, and then put it between his lips and lighted it. He leaned back in the padded chair and stared up at the ceiling, watching the blue-grey smoke swirl sluggishly upwards.

This suite of offices was above the mask shop. The entire property belonged to him, including the restaurant. It wasn't in his name, but he was the owner. The mask shop was rented to an old man named Byles, who had no idea what other uses it was put to after he left in the evening. The box containing the radio equipment was, Byles had been told, a patent fire alarm that on no account was to be touched. He was an incurious old man, absorbed in his work of mask making and waxen figures. His business, though not a large one, was fairly profitable. He had contracts with several companies, who took most of his output. He had been a tenant when Barney had bought the premises from the previous owner, and had been allowed to remain. It would have been difficult to find a more suitable occupant.

Barney finished his cigarette, stubbed out the butt in the ashtray, and pressed the switch of the intercom. 'I'll do the letters, now,' he said.

His secretary, a plain woman with large shell-rimmed glasses, came in with her notebook, and for the next half-hour he was busy dictating letters concerning the agency.

'Sign them for me,' he said when he

had finished. 'I shall be leaving in a few minutes.'

'Yes, Mr. Barney,' she said, and went back to the outer office. He heard the clicking of the typewriter, turned the key in the lock, and picked up a pigskin briefcase from a chair. It was empty, and he transferred the money he had received from Delmar from the desk drawer to the briefcase.

In his unpretentious house at Surbiton, there was a safe built into the wall of the bedroom that was considerably larger than most of its kind. The contents would have been cheap at five hundred thousand pounds, for in it was the bulk of the proceeds from his nefarious deals over a long period. Barney believed in fluid assets that were available immediately at any hour of the day or night. There was a considerable sum in cash, but the majority of the fortune he had amassed was in diamonds. They took up less room, and their value remained fairly static. He had contacts in Amsterdam and Hatton Garden who kept him supplied with the stones whenever he required them.

Large sums of money in cash paid into a bank might cause someone to wonder about its source. Barney was taking no risks of this kind. When the time came to give up the game, he could take his diamonds and disappear abroad, where he would be able to live in luxury for the rest of his life. At present, he lived on the profits from the agency, keeping well within that limit. It required stringent self-control, for he was a man who liked the good things of life, but he had no wish to make people curious. Nobody could say: 'How does Rodney Barney manage to live like that on the money he makes?' His accounts were scrupulously kept. His income returns for tax were unquestionable.

Twice, he had come near to disaster. The time when Fielding had tried to arrest him on the stretch of road in the country after they had made a deal. He hadn't been prepared for that. Fielding had fooled him completely. If only he hadn't been so impatient ... But he had taken quick action and the danger was averted.

The second time had been the outcome of the death of the man Hyams. He had got too curious. He had nearly succeeded in establishing the connection between Barney and the head of the organization of which he was a part. The 'accident' had saved the situation, but Hyams had mentioned something to Vanya that had made her suspicious. She had started to ask awkward questions. Well, that danger, too, had been dealt with.

He closed the briefcase, put on his hat and coat, and passed into the outer office. He said good night to his secretary, who was busily typing the letters he had given her, and went down the narrow stairs to the street.

He took a taxi to Waterloo. His own car, fitted with the two-way radio, was in the garage at his house. He seldom used it to travel back and forth to his office. Parking was too difficult, and he had no wish to leave it open to the possible curious prying of a garage assistant. On the occasions when he kept his appointments, always at different places, he hired cars, again always from different garages. In this way, he hoped that he had completely covered his tracks.

He was unmarried. There had at one time been a Mrs. Barney, but she had long since passed into the realm of the forgotten, and his small house was looked after by an elderly housekeeper who thought her employer was a model of everything that a man should be. Household bills were paid promptly, his habits were regular, and he wasn't finicky over his food. He enjoyed good, plain cooking, and never kept a meal waiting. If he was unable to get home, he would telephone in plenty of time. Mrs. Grayle had no cause for complaint.

He arrived home just after five o'clock, letting himself in with his latch-key. Mrs. Grayle, grey-haired and neat, came out of the kitchen as he entered the small hall. 'You're early today, sir,' she said, greeting him with a smile. 'Would you like some tea?'

'Thank you, Mrs. Grayle,' he said, taking off his hat and overcoat and hanging them on the hallstand. 'I should, very much.'

'I've made some scones,' she said. 'They're hot — straight out of the oven. I'll bring the tea into the lounge in about five minutes, sir.'

She disappeared again into the kitchen, and he went upstairs to his bedroom. Here, he opened the safe and put the money from the briefcase inside, closing the door again. Even Mrs. Grayle was not aware of its existence, and would have been dismayed could she have seen the contents, for she did not regard her employer as a particularly rich man.

He went into the bathroom, washed his hands, and made his way down to the lounge. A coal fire was burning cheerfully — the housekeeper did not approve of gas or electric fires, considering them expensive and less comfortable — and a tray had been set on a low table in front of it. The hot scones, with butter and jam, were flanked by a generously sized teapot, with milk and sugar, and the special cup and saucer to which he was particularly addicted. It was the only one left of a rather beautiful set of Rockingham china he had picked up one day in Berwick Market.

He had scarcely finished his tea when the telephone rang. He got up with a frown and picked up the receiver. A man's voice came over the wire, a voice that he did not immediately recognize.

'Is that Barney — Rodney Barney?' it inquired.

'Speaking,' answered Barney. 'Who's that?'

'This is Clint,' said the voice.

'Clint?' repeated Barney, and his face changed. 'I don't think I know anyone of that name.'

'Oh yes, you do,' broke in Clint. 'It's no good pretending. I know all about you.'

'I'm afraid you must have got the wrong number,' said Barney. 'I don't know any —'

'Come off it,' snapped Clint. 'It's no good, I tell you. I followed you the other night, after you'd met Felton on the Guildford Road.'

Barney's face hardened, but he still attempted to bluff. 'I haven't the least idea what you're talking about,' he said. 'I know nothing of anyone called Felton, nor have I been on the Guildford Road.'

'Listen,' said Clint curtly. 'I'm not going to talk on the telephone. I want to see you — tonight. Come to your office at eight o'clock. I'll meet you there. There's quite a lot I've got to say to you.'

'I shall do no such thing,' interrupted Barney. 'You must be mad.'

'Don't be a fool!' snarled Clint. 'You'll come.'

There was a click as he rang off. Barney stared at the receiver and then, slowly, he put it back on its rest. This was a development he had not expected. And it would have to be dealt with quickly.

Confound Clint! So he'd followed him, had he? How had he known about the appointment on the Guildford Road? Had Felton told him? No, that didn't seem very likely. It was more probable that Clint had followed Felton. That was it. He'd known that there was to be a meeting — Snow would have known because he had delivered the letter to Felton's flat. He'd have mentioned it to Clint or to Salvatori. The question was, had Clint told anyone else about his boss's identity? If blackmail was his object — and that seemed certain — he would be unlikely to spread his knowledge around. He'd keep it to himself.

Barney went out into the hall and called to his housekeeper. 'Would it be possible to have dinner a little earlier, Mrs. Grayle?' he asked apologetically. 'I'm afraid I have to go back to London unexpectedly.'

'What time would you like it, sir?' she asked.

Barney looked at his watch. It was already nearly six. 'On second thoughts, don't bother,' he said. 'I'll get a meal in town.'

'It will be no trouble,' she began, but he stopped her.

'No, no,' he said. 'I have to be there by eight. It would mean leaving here before seven. There wouldn't be time to eat in comfort.'

He went up to his bedroom and opened the safe. In a drawer at the bottom was a small automatic pistol and several clips of cartridges. He took out the pistol and examined it, pushing a clip into the butt. He pulled back the jacket so that there was a cartridge in the breech, and put on the safety catch. Then he slipped the little weapon into his pocket, went down again to the lounge, and poured himself out a drink. He was an abstemious man as a rule, and seldom drank spirits, but he felt that he needed the stiff brandy to counteract the effect of the shock he had received.

Perhaps this was the time he had been expecting one day — the time to quit. He had known that it must come sooner or later. Well, he was prepared for it. But he was not going to miss this last deal with Delmar that was worth money — more money than he had at first anticipated — if he could handle Felton in the right way, and that shouldn't be difficult. If he were going to quit, Felton would no longer be of any value. Why pay him a large sum for something that he might obtain for nothing?

In the train on the way to Waterloo, Barney pondered the matter. He was already a very wealthy man. One more good deal and he wouldn't mind calling it a day.

10

Clint said nothing about his discovery to Salvatori or any of the others in the group. This was his pigeon. He had taken all the trouble and the risk; and he didn't see why they should cash in on the result.

His plan had succeeded perfectly. He had followed the car containing the unknown, after the interview with Felton, to a garage at Esher. Here, the man had left the car and walked to a bus stop. It had been a little difficult to keep him in sight because the motorcycle was a hindrance, but Clint had managed it by pretending that the machine had broken down. He had no worries that the man he was following would recognize him. The crash helmet, plus goggles, took care of that.

He followed him to the house in Surbiton, and an inquiry at a public house had resulted in his obtaining the name of the person who lived there. Further inquiries led him to the agency over the mask shop, and the identity chain was complete. Clint was elated, or as near elated as his cold, unemotional nature ever allowed him to get. He was now in a position to dictate terms, and he meant to make them stiff. He saw the possibility of making a great deal of money. Nothing less than a lump sum down and fifty percent interest in all future deals was going to satisfy him, and he couldn't see that Barney could do anything but agree. Clint had him right where he wanted him.

He walked up the narrow stairs to the offices of Barney's Variety Agency at a few minutes after eight that evening, carrying a thin-bladed throwing knife up his sleeve with the handle nestling against his wrist, ready at a second's notice to be whipped out and used. It was Clint's favourite weapon, and he was an expert.

There was a light in the outer office when he reached the landing. He could see it shining through the half-glass door. He smiled — a barely perceptible curving of the thin lips, but the nearest he ever got to mirth. So Barney had come!

He opened the door, went in, and stood for a moment, his eyes shooting quickly and suspiciously round the office. He had no illusions concerning the man he was dealing with. The door to the inner office was partially open, and Clint stole silently over on rubber-soled shoes and peered in. Rodney Barney was sitting behind the big desk, smoking a cigar. He looked perfectly calm and collected. There was not a trace of concern on his big, bland face.

Clint kicked the door wide open. 'Well,' he said, 'so you came.'

'I was curious,' said Barney. He hadn't moved a muscle at the suddenness of Clint's entrance. 'I wanted to see you.'

'You're not still going to try that bluff?' said Clint. 'It won't work. I know you.'

'So you know, eh?' remarked Barney quietly. 'Well, what about it?'

'It makes things less one-sided, doesn't it? We're equal now.'

'Except that you haven't the brains,' retorted Barney contemptuously. 'Does anyone else know?'

'Do you think I'm a complete fool? This is between you and me.'

'I see.' Barney nodded. 'Well, what do you want?'

'I want a cash payment of twenty thousand pounds,' replied Clint promptly, 'and a bigger cut in future. Half.'

Barney stared at him. 'You must be out of your mind. Do you imagine for one single instant that I would agree to anything so ridiculous?'

'You can afford it. You must have made a huge profit.'

'That's got nothing to do with it. The expenses have been high.' He moved his hand casually towards a drawer in the desk.

As if by magic, the knife was in Clint's hand. 'Keep your hands on the desk in front of you,' he snapped. 'Otherwise … ' He made a significant movement with the knife.

Barney shrugged his shoulders. 'Let's be sensible about this,' he said. 'I am willing to listen to any reasonable request.'

'I've told you what I want,' said Clint, balancing the knife on his palm. 'That's what I'm taking. There are a lot of people who'd like to know who has been running this outfit — including the police.'

'Granted,' said Barney, with a broad smile that showed his teeth. 'They would also be interested in the name of the man who killed Vanya. They're still looking for him.'

'I didn't kill Fielding — or Hyams,' retorted Clint.

'That evens things up,' said Barney. 'You squeal on me, I squeal on you. Rather a deadlock, isn't it?'

'I can prove that Vanya was killed by your orders,' said Clint. 'Salvatori knows.'

'Yes, I suppose he does. It would seem that you may be holding a better hand than I thought. Perhaps, after all … '

He ducked suddenly. Clint flicked his wrist and the knife, flashing like a streak of lightning, flew over the desk. Had Barney been less quick, it would have caught him in the throat. But it passed harmlessly over his head, and before Clint had time to leap forward, the little automatic spat viciously. Clint stumbled, put his hand to his chest, coughed, and fell forward. His clawing fingers clutched at the edge of the desk but failed to grip, and he slid to the floor.

Barney came round from behind the desk and looked down at him. His face was quite expressionless. He moved the body with his foot, but it was quite limp. He put the automatic back in his pocket, went over to the door, and locked it. From a small cabinet in one corner of the office, he took out a bottle of Haig and poured out a fairly large drink. He drank it quickly, closed the cupboard, and came back to the desk. With a duster from a drawer, he carefully wiped the automatic, laid it down, and produced a sheet of brown paper and some string. With great care he placed the pistol on the sheet of paper and made it into a neat parcel, tying it with the string. Sitting down, he carefully wrote an address in block capitals, and surveyed his handiwork with satisfaction.

After a short pause, he got up and once more inspected the body of Clint. The man was quite dead. Two bullets had hit him in the chest, and one must have found the heart. There was very little blood; only a faint smear on the carpet.

Rodney Barney went to his overcoat and took a pair of gloves from the pocket. Putting these on, he came back, stooped over the body, and lifted it under the arms. He half-dragged, half-carried it over to the window, then went over and switched out the light. He could see dimly by the glow of a nearby electric sign that partially lit up the office with a reddish light. It was very faint, but enough to see what he had to do.

He opened the window. Near the sill, an iron fire-escape ran down to the yard below. Across the way he could see the back of the Eldorado. He raised the limp figure of Clint up onto the sill, pushed him as far out as he could, and let him go. The dull thud of the body as it struck the concrete of the yard came up to him. He listened for a moment, but there was no other sound, and he closed the window.

Everything so far had gone as he had planned. There was one more thing that must be done that night, and then he could go back home. He put on his hat and overcoat, unlocked the door, went into the outer office, and opened the door to the stairs. This he closed and locked behind him, and he went quickly down the narrow staircase to the street. In his pocket was the parcel he had made of the automatic. What he was going to do was a long shot. It might come off; but if it didn't, no harm would be done.

He walked round the corner to the

Eldorado and slowed as he came within sight of the entrance. The vestibule was brilliantly lighted but empty. There was no sign of the uniformed commissionaire. He had probably slipped away for a drink. It was the slack period.

Barney went quickly through the glass doors, took the parcel out of his pocket, and laid it down on the counter. This was the only risky moment. If he were seen …

But he wasn't. Nobody appeared, and he was outside again in less than a couple of seconds. At the corner of the street, he hailed a passing taxi and was driven to Waterloo.

11

The parcel was found by the commissionaire on his return from, as Barney had imagined, a drink which he was allowed to have at that hour of the evening. It was addressed to Salvatori, and the commissionaire took it up to the office.

Salvatori was sitting gloomily at his desk. He was immaculately dressed, as usual, with the white gardenia in his lapel, but this gay apparel was not reflected in his expression. 'It is for me?' he asked when the commissionaire handed him the parcel. 'Who left it 'ere?'

The commissionaire shook his head. 'I don't know, sir. It was on the counter when I came back from me break. I brought it up at once.'

Salvatori turned the little packet over in his plump hands. 'All right,' he said. 'You can go.'

The commissionaire withdrew, and the manager cut the string and tore open the wrapping. When he found the pistol, he uttered an exclamation of surprise and stared at it. He looked to see if there was any note in the packet, but there was nothing other than the automatic.

He held the pistol up to see if there was a name engraved on the butt, but again he found nothing to solve the mystery. Why should this weapon have been left for him? Was it a joke? Who would play such a trick?

Salvatori sniffed at the end of the short barrel. The pistol seemed to have been recently fired. He laid it down on the desk, feeling a little uneasy. He did not like firearms — particularly firearms that came from nowhere.

There was a tap on the door, and Mr. Snow came in. 'Have you seen Clint anywhere?' he asked.

'Clint?' Salvatori shook his head. 'No, I have not seen him tonight. You should not come 'ere.'

'I want to find Clint.'

''E is not 'ere,' said the manager. ''E 'as not been 'ere.'

Snow looked at him curiously. 'What's the matter?' he asked. 'You look worried.'

'I have cause for uneasiness,' said Salvatori. 'I do not like the way things are going. There is trouble about, yes? The killing of that woman 'ere — it was stupid. The police 'ave been in and out ever since. An' there was another woman. She was 'ere with that man Felton. Clint found 'er up here. She said she was looking for the ladies' room, but I am not sure. I do not like it at all.'

'You're always grumbling,' said Snow.

'I never wanted to be in this business,' declared Salvatori. 'I was 'appy with my restaurant. That is what I understand. I do not want to be mixed up with these other things.'

'I suppose he had some hold on you, eh?' said Snow. 'That applies to most of us, I think. He picked his people well, I must say that.'

The door opened suddenly, and Detective-Inspector Mason, followed by a uniformed sergeant, came in. 'Did you know that there is a dead man in the yard at the back of these premises?' asked Mason without preliminary.

Salvatori's fat face went pale. 'A dead man?' he almost squeaked.

Mason nodded. 'A man named Clint,' he answered. 'He worked here, I believe. He was shot.'

'When — when was this?' asked Salvatori, passing his tongue over suddenly dry lips.

'He was found a few minutes ago,' replied Mason. 'We got a tip-off that he was there. What do you know about it?'

'Me?' cried Salvatori. 'I know nothing.'

Mason's sharp eyes had seen the little automatic on the desk. Salvatori saw the direction of his glance and his heart gave a jump.

Mason picked up the gun delicately by the trigger guard. 'Where did you get this?' he asked, and his voice was stern.

'It is not mine,' declared Salvatori. 'I —'

'Whose is it? Yours?' Mason swung round on the astonished Snow.

'No, it's not mine,' answered Snow.

'This gun has been fired recently,' said the inspector.

Salvatori was on his feet, an agitated and frightened man. 'I know nothing about it,' he asserted. 'It was left 'ere, in a parcel.'

'Oh, yes?' said Mason sceptically. 'Who left it?'

'I don't know,' answered the manager. 'The commissionaire found it. It was addressed to me. 'E will tell you.'

'I've no doubt he will,' said Mason. 'We'll see him. I'll have this gun tested for prints.'

'You will find mine,' interrupted Salvatori excitedly. 'Of course you will. I 'andled it when I took it out of the wrapping. Look 'ere — this is the paper it was wrapped in.' He stooped and took the torn paper out of the waste-paper basket.

'I'll take that as well,' said the inspector. He wrapped the gun carefully in his handkerchief and put it in his pocket. 'Stay here, Sergeant, and keep an eye on these men. I'll be back shortly.'

'There's no need for me to stay, is there?' put in Snow. 'I don't know anything about — '

'I'm afraid you will have to wait here until I have completed my preliminary investigations,' said Mason. 'I shall want your name and address — give them to the sergeant, will you?'

He went out and hurried down the stairs. Making his way through the restaurant, eyed curiously by the staff, he passed out the back way into the yard. By the light of a powerful electric hand-lamp, a little group of people were bending over the body of Clint.

The divisional surgeon rose to his feet as Mason joined them. 'This man was shot twice in the chest,' he said. 'One of the bullets appears to have penetrated the heart. I can tell you more about that after the post-mortem. He hasn't been dead long — not more than two hours, in my opinion. There are signs of a struggle. It looks as though he'd been bashed about a bit. Again, we'll know more about that after I've examined the body with your pathologist.'

'Thanks, Doctor,' said Mason. He took one of the detectives aside. 'I want you to take this to headquarters and have it tested for dabs,' he said in a low voice. 'I think it's the murder weapon.' He took the gun carefully out of his pocket, still wrapped in the handkerchief, and gave it to the man. 'Handle it carefully,' he said, 'and be as quick as you can.' The man nodded and hurried away.

A sudden brilliant flash of light illuminated the yard as the police photographer took a picture of the body. It lit up starkly the bare yard and startled a cat that was perched on the top of the wall. Three more photographs from different angles were taken, and then Mason gave orders for the body to be removed.

The information that there was a dead man in the yard at the back of the Eldorado had come through on the telephone. The call had originated from a public call box at Waterloo station. The voice was a man's but was obviously disguised. He had probably spoken through a handkerchief stretched across the mouthpiece. Mason had been under the impression that the call was a hoax, but he had very soon discovered that it was nothing of the kind.

While he was waiting for the return of the man he had sent to have the gun tested, he interviewed the commissionaire. That startled man told him of the finding of the packet addressed to Salvatori in the vestibule, and how he had taken it up to the office at once. He had no idea who had left it. It had been his break-time, and he was away for ten minutes. Mason questioned the other members of the staff, getting them out one by one into the vestibule, but nobody had seen anyone leave the parcel.

It sounded as though the murderer, having shot Clint, had packed up the gun and left it in the vestibule. But there was the distinct possibility that Salvatori had done it himself. It seemed an idiotic thing to do, since it would have been easier to have got rid of the murder weapon or left it in the yard. Perhaps somebody was trying to involve Salvatori or confuse the issue, though the fact that the stout manager might have tried a kind of double bluff couldn't be entirely discounted. It depended a great deal on whether any fingerprints were found on the gun.

The report was not long in arriving, and Mason went back to the office to interview Salvatori again, primed with the fresh information that had reached him. The manager was sitting at his desk, fiddling with a pencil. The uniformed sergeant, stolid and silent, was standing near the door. Mr. Snow was sitting in a chair, trying to look unconcerned but not succeeding very well. They all looked at Mason when he came in.

'There are only one set of fingerprints on that pistol,' announced the inspector. 'I shall have to take yours, Mr. Salvatori, for comparison.'

Salvatori moistened his lips. 'I 'ave told you, they will be the same,' he said. 'I 'andled the pistol when I took it out of the parcel.'

He submitted quietly while Mason produced the inkpad he had sent for and took several prints of his fingertips. He compared them with the still-damp photographs of the prints found on the murder weapon. They were identical.

'There's no doubt that these are yours,' Mason said. 'And there are no others.'

'It is a trick — a frame-up!' declared Salvatori. 'I did not even know that Clint was dead.'

'That's as may be,' said Mason. 'I shall have to ask you to accompany me to the station and make a statement.'

'You cannot arrest me for this!' cried Salvatori, leaping to his feet. I 'ave told you the truth. I do not 'ave anything to do with it. It is as I say!'

'I'm not charging you with anything at

the moment,' said Mason. 'I'm detaining you for questioning.'

Salvatori appealed to Snow. 'You can tell 'im,' he cried. 'You can say that I know nothing about this.'

'You leave me out of it,' broke in Snow. 'I can't help you.'

'I shall need a statement from you as well,' interrupted Mason. 'You'd better come with us.'

'Now look here,' began Snow. 'I only — '

'You can reserve all that until we get to the station,' said the inspector. 'You will have ample opportunity of saying anything you wish to then.'

★   ★   ★

Rodney Barney read of the discovery of the murdered man in his evening newspaper, although he had heard about it when he reached his office the following morning. His secretary had been full of it. He wondered, with inward amusement, what she would say if she knew that the dead man had been shot in that office, and that her smiling employer had been responsible. But she had no suspicion of the fact. She would have been horrified at the mere suggestion, for she had always looked upon Mr. Barney as the nicest of men, kind and considerate, and had no knowledge of the real personality that lurked beneath his genial exterior.

Slade also read an account of the death of Clint and was not unduly surprised. Evidently he had succeeded in his object in discovering the unknown's identity, and swift action had been taken to ensure his silence. Slade wondered how it was that the body had come to be found in the yard at the back of the Eldorado. It would, he thought, have been more in keeping with previous methods adopted by the head of the group if it had been found by the side of some country road, but he concluded that the unknown must have had some very good reason.

That the man was utterly ruthless, there was no doubt. He had killed three times, and there might be other murders that the Ghost Squad knew nothing about. It was time, Slade decided, that something drastic was done.

The opportunity would come with this

fresh deal. This time Hallowes must arrange to have road blocks set up as soon as the quarry reached the meeting-place, and police hidden close by, ready to close in at a given signal. The quicker Slade got the fake information about the defence in the event of nuclear war, the better; for the man must be taken in the act, otherwise he might easily slip through their fingers. Unless he was caught with the evidence on him, a clever lawyer could tear the case against him to shreds.

That evening at a little after nine o'clock, the telephone rang. As Slade put the receiver to his ear, the voice that by now was so familiar came over the wire. 'Is that Felton?'

'Yes,' answered Slade.

'You recognize my voice?'

'Yes.'

'Circumstances have compelled me to alter certain plans. I shall require that information as soon as possible.'

'I'll do my best,' said Slade.

'When do you think you will have it available?'

Slade thought for a moment. If he said

he could get it too quickly, the other might get suspicious. 'I'll try and have it in three days' time,' he said.

'You cannot possibly get it any quicker?'

'I might,' said Slade. 'It depends on several things. I can't force an opportunity.'

'I understand. In order to save time, we will dispense with the usual routine. I will telephone you at this hour in three days' time —'

'Suppose I have it sooner?'

There was a moment's silence. 'I will telephone in two days,' said the voice, and the man rang off.

Slade put down the receiver thoughtfully. Something was causing the unknown to panic. Was it the death of Clint? It was more likely that the discovery of his identity by the dead man had shaken him. He must be wondering whether Clint had passed on what he had discovered to any of the rest of the group, and was preparing to close down the outfit. It was lucky, thought Slade, that he hadn't already got this last piece of information that he evidently so badly wanted. If the Clint business had done nothing else, it had proved that the system wasn't as watertight as its creator had imagined.

These things tended to run well for a time, but there was always the human element to be taken into consideration, which was unpredictable. Slade had seen more schemes fail because someone had decided to act out of step than because there was anything lacking in their original conception. People couldn't be treated as puppets. They had minds of their own, and they usually started to use them at the wrong moment, believing that their way was better.

The following morning, Slade saw Hallowes and brought that cool and efficient man up to date. Hallowes had already seen what had happened to Clint and put two and two together. 'It looks as though you'll shortly be on another assignment, Slade,' he said, puffing happily at his inevitable pipe. 'This business ought to be in the bag pretty soon.'

Slade grinned. 'I suppose you've got it all planned, eh?' he said. 'What am I going to be this time?'

'One thing at a time. Let's get this over

first. I'll get in touch with Special Branch and they can start a plan of operations. The actual arrest of this feller will be their pigeon. As soon as you let me know the location of the interview, they can go into action.'

'Impress on them not to make any move until after he leaves me,' said Slade. 'I don't want to be a casualty in this, and he's quite capable of putting a bullet through me if he gets the slightest inkling that it's a trap.'

Hallowes peered into the bowl of his pipe. 'Don't worry; every precaution will be taken. We don't want to lose you, you know. You're too valuable.'

'Never mind the compliments. Just make sure that everything goes smoothly. Now, about this defence plan. When can I have it? When he phones me next, I'd like to be able to say I've got it.'

'You will,' answered Hallowes. 'I'll get on to it right away.'

Shortly after, Slade took his leave. It seemed that the case, so far as he was concerned, was nearly over. The rest would be taken over by Special Branch. This was the usual procedure. The members of the Ghost Squad never appeared in court. Their job ended with the undercover work. Their testimony was taken down and used to prepare the brief for the public prosecutor to take action. By the time the case came up in court, Slade would be busy on another. It might take him a week, a month, or a year. Perhaps he could wangle a little leave in between. He felt tired.

★ ★ ★

The murder of Clint had caused an upheaval in the organization which had, hitherto, run so smoothly. The smaller fry, who did not know Clint or Salvatori, were not affected; but the others, who had taken their instructions from the dead man or the restaurant manager, began to see the red light. Among these was Mr. Snow.

He had gone to the station with Salvatori and Inspector Mason, but he hadn't been detained very long. He had no information to offer regarding the murder, and he succeeded in convincing Mason of this. He left the police station with the firm intention of getting out of the group while the going was good.

Salvatori was not so lucky. For nearly three hours he was subjected to a barrage of questions. The murder of Vanya was still fresh in Mason's mind, and he sensed a possible connection between the killing of Clint and the death of the singer. It was only by the slightest margin that Salvatori escaped being charged with Clint's murder. The evidence of the commissionaire that he *had* taken the parcel up was the thing that saved him. It instilled that element of doubt that decided Mason against an immediate arrest. It was possible that there might have been an attempt at a frame-up, as Salvatori reiterated. That frightened man was allowed to go in the small hours of the morning, but a tail was put on him as a matter of routine precaution.

'I don't think he did it,' said the weary Mason, gulping a cup of coffee his sergeant had brought from the canteen. 'There's no motive for one thing, and for another I don't think he's got the guts.'

'It looks to me like a gang killing,' said the sergeant.

'You've been reading too many thrillers,' grunted Mason. 'We'll probably find there

182

was some woman or other involved.' He was a bachelor, and it was his favourite dictum that a woman was at the bottom of most crimes. 'We'd better get some rest while we can.'

Rodney Barney paid a visit that evening to the Orpheum Theatre, where the Great Delmar was entertaining a fascinated audience with feats of magic that brought increasing applause. He came into his dressing-room after his turn to find Barney awaiting him.

'Ah, it is you, my friend,' he said, sitting down before his dressing-table and beginning to remove his make-up. 'You have news for me, yes?'

'I expect to have what you want either tomorrow or the day after,' said Barney.

'That is good. I am anxious to complete this business, my friend.'

'So am I. It will be the last deal between us, Delmar.'

The magician looked at him quickly. 'Something has happened?'

'I've decided to give it up,' answered Barney.

The thin lips curled into a faint smile.

'This sudden decision has nothing to do with the death of that man — what was his name, Clint?' asked Delmar. 'I read an account of it in the papers. He was found in a yard below your office.'

Barney looked at him coolly. 'Maybe,' he replied evasively. 'But one cannot go on forever. There must come a time when it is good policy to stop.'

'While it is possible, yes?' said Delmar. 'Perhaps you are wise, my friend. Me — I think sometimes that I shall soon be returning to my own country.'

'You will be welcome, I'm sure. You have been of great service to your government.'

'I have done some of the things I came to do,' said Delmar. 'In the event of war, I shall have contributed a little towards ensuring a victory.'

'A war would be disastrous for both sides,' said Barney. 'I think that such a thing would be madness.'

Delmar shrugged his shoulders. 'People *are* mad,' he said. 'I speak to you freely. Can you call people sane who spend millions on preparing their own destruction? It is not possible, my friend. It is the action of the insane. The world has become a madhouse.'

'Yet you are prepared to assist in this destruction.'

'I do what I am paid to do, my friend. As you do. I cannot prevent these mad people rushing to annihilation. Only the peoples of the world could do that. But they are too busy with their own affairs, with their petty strikes for more and more money, with their pre-occupation with all the things that do not matter because they will be useless in face of the disaster that could overtake them at any moment. They are like stupid children, my friend, who play on the brink of a volcano. One day it will erupt, and the molten lava will engulf them.' He wiped the greasepaint from his face with a towel, got up, and went over to the wash-basin, turning on the hot tap. 'There is a saying, my friend,' he went on, 'that those whom the gods would destroy, they first make mad. I think that is very true.'

Barney took out his case and helped himself to a cigarette. 'I hope,' he remarked as he flicked his lighter into flame and dipped the end of the cigarette into it, 'that this will not happen in our lifetime. I am looking forward to enjoying my retirement.'

'You, my friend, are concerned only with yourself,' said Delmar, washing his face and hands in the basin and drying them on a towel that hung nearby.

'Aren't you?'

'No.' Delmar shook his head. 'I would like to see a peaceful world. I would like all this suspicion between nations to end. You are surprised at that, yes?'

'I never guessed you were a sentimentalist,' said Barney, with a slight sneer in his voice.

'Perhaps I am a realist. I know that this is something that can never happen — not in these days. Progress, my friend, is a word that no longer means progressing. Our scientists have made wonderful discoveries, yes. But they have not progressed — they have gone backwards. To progress must be to *benefit*, not to *destroy*. It must not concern itself with better and bigger bombs; it must concern itself with an attitude of mind, which would render such things unnecessary. You do not understand me?'

'I understand you,' said Barney. *This man*, he thought, *is a fanatic. He should be on an orange box in the park, preaching, instead of working as a foreign agent, a spy buying secret information for his country.* He failed to understand that Delmar was only carrying out his duty as he conceived it.

Delmar, guessing what was passing through his mind, smiled. 'What I do,' he said, as he put on his tie, 'is for the benefit of my country, my friend. What you do is to benefit yourself.'

'You get paid for what you do, don't you?' said Barney.

'Yes, and I get paid well. But it does not stop me being able to think.'

'We don't look at things in the same way. I'll let you know as soon as I am in possession of the information you want. Have the cash ready.'

'It is waiting,' said Delmar.

★ ★ ★

The roll of microfilm reached Slade on the afternoon of the day when the unknown had said he would ring in the evening. The bait was ready. All that was necessary now was for the fish to rise to it, and be hooked.

Slade found that the time passed slowly. He was impatient, now that everything was set for the finale, to get it over and done with. He hoped that there would be no slip-up. Once Special Branch took over, it was out of his hands. If anything went wrong, it would be their responsibility, not his. But he couldn't help feeling excited at the result.

As it drew nearer to the time for the unknown to make his telephone call, Slade became more and more restless. He paced up and down the lounge of the flat, smoking cigarette after cigarette, until the ashtrays were full of butts and his mouth felt hot and dry.

He wondered what locality would be chosen this time. It would be somewhere in the country, unless the usual routine was altered. A stretch of deserted road some-where that would give Special Branch an opportunity to place their men. Cars would close in from each end, and there would be no possibility of the unknown escaping. And the evidence would be on him — the microfilm that he had just bought from

Slade. There was no way he would be able to get out of the trap.

The telephone rang. Slade went quickly to the instrument and picked up the receiver. The voice he had been expecting reached his ears.

'Felton?'

'Yes.'

'Well?'

'I've got what you want.'

'Excellent.' The voice was not quite its usual monotonous self. 'You can bring it to me tonight?'

Slade thought quickly. Would he have time to get the location through to Hallowes? And, more importantly, would Hallowes have time to brief Special Branch? 'I don't know about tonight,' he said. 'Can't you make it tomorrow?'

'It's only nine-thirty,' said the voice impatiently. 'You could meet me at midnight. That will give you plenty of time.'

Two and a half hours, thought Slade. *It should be long enough.* 'Where?' he asked.

'There's a farm called Haytree on the Portsmouth Road. Just beyond it, on the right, there are three oak trees. You can't mistake them. They are the only trees at that spot, and they grow in the shape of a triangle. Be there at midnight.'

'All right,' agreed Slade. 'Bring the money.'

'I shall have it with me,' said the voice. Slade heard the click as he rang off.

There was no time to lose. He dialled Hallowes's private number, but the superintendent was not at home. Neither was he at his office in Scotland Yard, or at the shop in Clapham. It was a contingency that he had not taken into account. Of course, Hallowes had not been prepared for such quick action on the part of the unknown. He had expected that the appointment would be made for the following night.

Slade lit a cigarette and wondered what the best thing to do was. He could get through to the officer in charge of Special Branch and explain the situation, trusting that they would be ready to go into action. He decided that this was his only course.

He got through to Scotland Yard and was connected with the man he sought, and explained the situation. He discovered that Hallowes had already made the necessary arrangements. Special Branch were all ready, and only waiting to receive the location of the meeting and the signal to go ahead.

Slade put down the receiver with a feeling of relief. It would be all right. The plan would go through. He helped himself to a large Haig, which he drank neat, and prepared for his excursion. It was a clear, frosty night, like the other had been, and he made his way by train and bus to the nearest point from which he could walk the rest of the journey to the rendezvous.

He found Haytree Farm, and a little further on the three oak trees. They grew in a rough triangle by the edge of the road and were unmistakable. By this time it was a quarter to twelve. The road at this spot was dark and deserted. There was no sound to break the silence. Although there were no other trees here, a short distance further along they grew thickly on both sides, almost meeting overhead, and formed a dark tunnel of interlaced branches.

There was no sign of the Special Branch men. If they had arrived, they were well hidden. Slade hoped fervently that they had.

He was beginning to feel a vague uneasiness that something was going to upset the plan.

He paced up and down by the oak trees, fingering the little packet containing a roll of microfilm in his pocket. An owl hooted close at hand, and he heard a sudden flurry of wings as it flew from one of the trees above his head to the others further along.

The minutes dragged slowly by. He was certain that it must be well past midnight, but a glance at his watch showed him that it was only five minutes to the hour. He lighted a cigarette and inhaled the soothing smoke gratefully. His nerves, usually calm, were jumpy. He would be glad when this business was over.

At last, on the still, cold air of the night, he heard, faintly in the distance, a clock strike. He counted the strokes — twelve — and compared the time with his watch. It wouldn't be long now ...

Five past twelve and nothing happened. No car appeared on the dark stretch of road; no sound of one approaching. A quarter past twelve.

The unknown had always been punctual. Why was he late? Surely he couldn't have expected a trap? There was no reason why he should. Something must have happened to delay him. Perhaps the car had broken down — a flat tyre? These things happened unexpectedly and could not be taken into account.

Half past twelve. The dark road stretched left and right of him, silent and deserted.

A quarter to one.

Slade decided to wait until one o'clock and then give it up. The unknown, for some reason or other, had altered his plans. There was no doubt that this was the right place. He hadn't made a mistake in the location.

A sound behind him made him turn swiftly. The figure of a man loomed up out of the darkness. 'Special Branch,' came a low whisper. 'You're Inspector Slade?'

'Yes,' said Slade.

'Something gone wrong?'

'It looks like it,' answered Slade. 'I can't understand what can have happened, but it doesn't seem as though our man is coming.'

'Are you going to wait?' asked the Special Branch detective.

Slade looked at his watch. It was now one o'clock. It was unlikely that the unknown would put in an appearance now. 'No,' he answered. 'We may as well give it up for tonight. I expect that I shall be hearing something — an explanation; a fresh appointment. He couldn't possibly have got wind of our plan to take him. There's probably quite a simple reason why he didn't come.'

'If you're going back, you may as well come with us,' said the other. 'It'll save you a lot of trouble.'

Slade was cold and a little depressed. He welcomed the offer of travelling in the comparative comfort of one of the police cars.

He was dropped, at his own request, some distance from his flat. The place might be watched, and he didn't want to arrive in an unmistakable police car. He took a taxi for the remaining part of the journey, and wearily climbed the staircase to his flat. He reached the landing, and was searching for his key, when a man stepped out of the shelter of an angled wall.

'I've been waiting for you, Mr. Felton,' said Barney softly. 'I'm sorry that you had your journey for nothing, but I was compelled to change my plans.'

12

Slade recognized the man who had spoken with something of a shock. This had been the man who had been dining with the blonde woman in the Eldorado on the night that Vanya had been murdered. There was no mistaking the dark-featured, good-looking face. And this was the head of the group — the owner of the voice that had spoken to him so often.

Slade put his key in the lock and turned it. 'You'd better come in,' he said.

'Thank you,' answered Barney. He followed Slade into the hall. 'I'm afraid that I put you to a lot of inconvenience.'

'What happened?' asked Slade, shutting the front door. This was something he had not bargained for. He would have to play this very carefully. There was no way he could notify Special Branch of his circumstances. He was on his own.

'I had trouble with my car,' explained Barney easily, but Slade sensed that the explanation was untrue. It was for some other reason that this man had chosen to change the place of the meeting to Slade's flat.

'I wondered why you didn't turn up,' said Slade. 'Come into the lounge.'

'I can't stay very long,' said Barney. 'We will get our business completed and then I must go.'

Slade took off his overcoat and threw it over a chair. His brain was working rapidly to find some way of dealing with the situation. He knew the identity of the unknown now. At least he knew what he looked like, though he still didn't know his name.

'You'll have a drink?' he said, going over to the sideboard and picking up the bottle of Haig.

Barney shook his head. 'No, thank you,' he replied. 'But don't let me stop you. I expect you're cold after your journey.'

Slade poured himself out a small whisky and squirted in a splash of soda. He saw that the man was carrying a briefcase. It looked full, and he concluded that he had brought the money with him.

'You have the film?' asked Barney. 'It will

not take long to make the exchange. Five thousand is what we agreed on, I think.'

Slade shook his head. He must play for time, time to evolve a scheme for holding this man. Once he left the flat, he might slip through their fingers for good. The trouble was that Slade was unarmed. Like the majority of police officers, he seldom carried firearms, and he was pretty certain that the man before him was not only armed but would have no hesitation in shooting his way out, if it became necessary.

'I want more than that,' Slade said.

Barney looked up from unfastening the briefcase. 'How much?' he demanded.

'Double. What I have is worth ten thousand.'

'That is a lot of money,' said Barney. 'Show me the film.'

Slade went over to his coat and took the packet from the pocket. He stripped off the covering and held up the roll of film. 'There you are,' he said, and stopped. In the other man's hand was an automatic, and it was pointing steadily at him.

'As I said,' Barney remarked coolly, 'ten thousand pounds is a lot of money.'

'Put that thing away,' broke in Slade. 'What do you think you're playing at?'

'I am not playing,' retorted Barney. 'I have no intention of paying you anything, Felton.'

'So that's your game, is it?'

'There's more to it than that. I had a particular reason for coming here, as you will see. Give me the film.'

Slade hesitated. He was in a tight corner, and he knew it. This man meant to kill him. That was his reason for coming to the flat.

'Give me the film,' repeated Barney.

Slade held out the little roll. Instead of taking it, Barney suddenly and completely unexpectedly gripped his wrist and gave it a jerk forward. The roll of film flew out of Slade's hand as he stumbled forward. Barney dropped the pistol and brought the edge of his hand down across the back of Slade's neck in a judo cut. Slade crumpled, fell to the floor, and lay still.

Barney picked up the automatic and put it in his pocket. Then he retrieved the roll of film, examined it swiftly, and pocketed that too. Stooping, he lifted the unconscious Slade under his armpits and dragged him out into the hall. Leaving him there, Barney went over to three doors that opened off the hall and found what he was looking for — the little kitchen. Going back to Slade, he pulled him across the floor and into the room. There was a gas cooker in one corner, and Barney opened the door to the oven. With a little trouble, he managed to get Slade's head and shoulders inside. Then he turned on the gas.

He paused for a moment to wipe his damp face, and then he carefully wiped the tap to remove his fingerprints. He stood for a moment looking down at the senseless figure with its head in the oven. He could hear the hissing of the gas. Before he could recover from the judo cut, the gas fumes would overcome him, thought Barney. When he was found, it would be put down to suicide. It would eventually be discovered that he had been stealing important information from his work place, and the police would conclude that that was the motive.

Barney went back to the lounge, after switching out the kitchen light. He looked round to make sure that he had overlooked nothing that might suggest there had been anyone there except the man who now lay in the kitchen. He put on his gloves, picked up the briefcase, and went over to the door. Just as he went out, the telephone began to ring. The sudden sound startled him for a moment. He looked at the instrument, smiled, and went out, switching off the light as he did so. He could smell the gas strongly as he opened the front door, and made sure that there was nobody about before he stepped quickly out onto the landing.

As he closed the front door gently behind him, he could hear the telephone still ringing.

* * *

'I think he'll do now,' said the doctor, getting up from his knees and dusting his trousers. 'It was touch and go, though. I was afraid at first that we were too late.'

Hallowes looked down at Slade. He was still unconscious, and breathing stertorously. His face was livid and his lips blue.

'We ought to get him into bed,' said the doctor. 'Will you help me carry him into the bedroom?'

Hallowes nodded. Between them they carried the limp form of Slade into the bedroom, undressed him, and got him into bed.

'I'll send along a nurse,' said the doctor. 'He'll need looking after for a day or two.' He was the divisional surgeon, and Hallowes had explained the situation without mentioning Slade's exact status.

The superintendent's arrival at the flat had been opportune. He had arrived home to learn that Slade had been trying to contact him urgently, and had tried to ring him at the flat but got no answer. A call to the Yard had resulted in his learning of Slade's call to Special Branch earlier, and the reason for it. He had learned of the result and tried to ring Slade again at his flat. Still getting no reply, he had decided to go there himself. When he arrived, the smell of gas was strong on the landing. Hallowes had smashed one of the panels of the front door and found Slade with, as he learned later, only a few seconds to spare.

He had telephoned to the nearest police station, and they had got in immediate touch with the divisional surgeon. In the meanwhile, Hallowes had got Slade away from the gas-filled kitchen and started artificial respiration, which the doctor had continued on his arrival. If Hallowes had not arrived when he did, Slade would have been dead. He had a fair idea of what had happened, but he couldn't do anything further until Slade had recovered his senses and was able to give an account.

The nurse, a competent woman, arrived just as it was getting light, and took complete charge of the flat. She made coffee for herself and Hallowes, settled her patient more comfortably, and awaited his return to consciousness.

Hallowes elected to remain. It was essential that he should have Slade's statement as soon as possible. The man they were after, indeed had so very nearly succeeded in catching, might very easily get away after all unless Slade could provide some clue to his identity.

Slade came back to consciousness slowly. He had been as near to death as he was ever likely to be. Almost as soon as he opened his eyes, he was violently sick. The cyanised condition of his face gradually faded to a more normal hue. The nurse made him some strong black coffee, and in an hour he was sitting up against the pillows, still feeble and with a splitting headache, but almost himself again. Weakly, and with many pauses, he explained to Hallowes what had happened.

'He was the man who was dining at the next table, was he?' said the superintendent. 'Did Lydia see him?'

Slade started to nod and winced.

'She'd be able to recognize him?' said Hallowes.

'Yes.' The words were faint and slightly blurred.

'We should be able to find out his name,' said Hallowes. 'If he's a regular frequenter of the Eldorado, the head waiter will probably know it.' He got to his feet. 'Now, you take it easy. I'll get on with this.'

He nodded a farewell and left. Slade closed his eyes to ease the throbbing in his head and fell asleep.

★ ★ ★

The head waiter at the Eldorado was helpful. He listened to what Hallowes had to say and wrinkled his forehead. 'A dark gentleman, sir,' he repeated thoughtfully, 'with a fair lady? Now, let me see ... I think that would be Mr. Barney. He doesn't come here a lot, but I recollect that he was here on the evening you mention. He's in the theatrical business, sir. He supplied us with our new singer — and Vanya too, poor woman.'

'Where does Mr. Barney live?' asked Hallowes.

'I don't know, but he has offices in the next street — over the shop that sells carnival masks and waxen figures.'

'Thank you,' said Hallowes.

A few minutes later he was climbing the stairs to the offices of Barney's Variety Agency. In the outer office he found a woman typing at a desk and put his inquiry.

'Mr. Barney isn't here today,' she answered. 'Is there something I can do?'

'I should like his private address,' said Hallowes.

'I'm sorry, I can't give you that,' she said. 'If you'd like to leave your name ... ?'

Hallowes produced his warrant card, and her face changed. 'Is anything the matter?' she asked quickly.

'I just want a word with Mr. Barney,' he answered. 'When did you last see him?'

'Yesterday afternoon. I expected him in this morning.'

'You haven't heard from him?' cut in Hallowes.

She shook her head and replied in the negative.

'Doesn't he usually let you know if he isn't coming to the office?'

'Well, yes he does,' she said, frowning. 'But it's very seldom that he stays away.'

'Is the inner office locked?' inquired Hallowes, and she nodded. 'Have you a key?'

'No; Mr. Barney is the only one who has a key.'

'Give me his private address,' said Hallowes, and this time she made no demur. 'Can I use your phone?' He took off the receiver without waiting for her permission and dialled divisional headquarters. 'Superintendent Hallowes speaking,' he said. 'I want two men sent round here right away, please.' He gave the address and rang off.

Within four minutes they had arrived, and Hallowes issued his instructions. 'You will stay here,' he said, 'and detain Rodney Barney for questioning if he shows up. Though I doubt if he will.'

'What about me?' asked the woman in alarm.

'You will stay here and tell anybody else who comes that your employer is away,' said Hallowes. 'I shall probably want to see you again later.'

He left the offices and was driven swiftly to Surbiton. He stopped at the police station to pick up two plain-clothes men, and went on to the address that the woman had given him.

'Mr. Barney?' he said to the elderly woman who opened the door.

'Mr. Barney is not at home,' she replied.

'We're police officers,' explained Hallowes. 'Can we come in?'

'What do you want?'

'The answer to a few questions,' replied Hallowes, and she invited him reluctantly into the hall. 'Are you Mrs. Barney?'

'Mr. Barney isn't married,' she answered.

'I'm his housekeeper, Mrs. Grayle. What are you here for? Is anything the matter?'

'I'm afraid there may be quite a lot the matter,' said the superintendent gravely. 'When did Mr. Barney leave?'

'It was late last night,' she answered. 'I did not know he had gone until I read the note he left this morning.'

'May I see it, please?'

'If you wait a moment, I'll fetch it. It's in the kitchen.'

Hallowes made a sign to one of the men with him. Quietly he followed the housekeeper to the kitchen door. When she came back, she held in her hand a half-sheet of notepaper. 'Here you are,' she said.

The note was very brief. *I have been called away,* it ran, *on unexpected business. I shall probably be away for some time.* It was signed with the initials 'R.B.'

'You have no idea where Mr. Barney has gone?' said Hallowes.

Mrs. Grayle shook her head. 'I don't understand. What is this all about?'

'I'm afraid we want Mr. Barney on rather a serious charge,' said Hallowes, and she stared at him in astonishment.

'There must be some mistake,' she said. 'Mr. Barney wouldn't do anything wrong.'

'That's as may be, but I shall have to ask you to let us search the house.'

'Well, really, I don't know that —'

'If you refuse,' said Hallowes, 'I shall get a search warrant. Meanwhile, I shall have to leave these two officers on the premises. It would save time if you agreed to the search.'

She hesitated, frowning. 'Very well,' she said at length. 'I'm quite sure that Mr. Barney has nothing to hide.'

They began a meticulous search of the whole house. There was a desk in the lounge, but it contained nothing but some envelopes and printed stationery. A pile of black ash in the grate suggested that a quantity of paper had been burnt, and Hallowes concluded that Barney had cleared the desk of anything important before leaving. There was nothing else of interest. The burnt ashes would have to be carefully collected and sent to the laboratory at the Yard in case they could bring up anything that might provide a clue to Barney's whereabouts.

In the bedroom they discovered, with the aid of Mrs. Grayle, that a large suitcase and a small dressing bag were missing. Shirts, underclothes, and two suits had also been taken, together with two pairs of pyjamas. It took them some time to find the safe, which was concealed behind a tallboy. The door was further covered by a panel that had been papered over to match the surrounding wall. It had been done so well that it wasn't visible to a casual glance. The safe was locked.

Hallowes sent for the housekeeper. 'Do you know what your employer kept in here?' he asked.

Mrs. Grayle looked so astonished at the sight of the safe that he was pretty sure this was the first time she had known of its existence.

She confirmed this. 'I never knew there was a safe there,' she said. 'No, I've no idea what Mr. Barney kept in it.'

'We shall have to get an expert to open it,' remarked the superintendent when she had gone. 'I doubt if there'll be anything in it, though.'

By the time they had gone over the entire house, they had collected nothing of any value for their pains. The car was missing from the garage, and Hallowes was able to get a description of it from the housekeeper. It was a black Jaguar of a not very new model, and she thought the number was PX 701, but of this she couldn't be sure.

Hallowes left her very worried but convinced that her employer could do no wrong. One of the detectives he had brought with him was left on guard in case Barney should try and communicate with his home — a contingency that Hallowes regarded as very unlikely but had to be provided for.

A description of the car and Rodney Barney was circulated, and Hallowes went back to see how Slade was getting on. He found him attired in a dressing-gown and sitting in front of the electric fire in the lounge, a fact of which the nurse most strongly disapproved.

'He insisted on getting up,' she said. 'He should have stayed in bed. I won't be responsible for any ill effects that ensue. I warned him, but he wouldn't take any notice.'

'I'm not feeling so bad now,' said Slade. 'Don't worry — if anything serious happens to me, I promise I won't blame you.'

She sniffed. 'You are an extremely wilful young man,' she declared. 'I'm glad I'm not your wife.'

Slade decided that he was glad too, but he thought it would be more tactful not to say so.

Hallowes told him the latest news.

'He must have planned his getaway carefully,' said Slade. 'I suppose it was this business with Clint that decided him to drop the whole set-up.'

'He'll have a job to get out of the country, if that is what he intends to do,' said Hallowes. 'All airports and ports are being watched, and every private airline has been notified. We'll get him.'

Slade looked dubious. 'You won't find him so easily,' he said. 'He's not a fool, you know. He's probably had this all worked out for a long time. He'd have planned his escape route in case of an emergency.' He settled back in his chair more comfortably. 'At any rate, I'm out of it,' he remarked complacently. 'My job's finished.'

Hallowes regarded him thoughtfully as he filled his pipe. 'Don't be too sure of that,' he said.

'Oh, come now,' protested Slade. 'What can I do now?'

'Well, that rather depends on how things go. You may be in at the death yet.'

'Whose?'

'Not yours this time,' said the superintendent, and added: 'I hope!'

★ ★ ★

'The Great Delmar' occupied a small but comfortable furnished flat in a turning off the Tottenham Court Road. He was a bachelor and attended to his own needs, except for a cleaner who came in for an hour each morning to tidy the two rooms and the small bathroom and kitchen, and make the bed. He had most of his meals at a small restaurant below the flat, only using the kitchen to cook his breakfast and brew himself tea or coffee.

He was a quiet man who occupied his time, when he was not at the theatre, in reading. When he was out of London working in one of the provincial theatres, the flat was shut; although the cleaner, who had a key, came regularly to keep it dusted.

Quite apart from the fact that his profession offered an excellent cover for his real activities, he was genuinely interested in conjuring. His bookshelves contained volumes on the subject, from the latest works to ancient books whose covers were tattered and stained. He spent a lot of time browsing in old bookshops in the hope of adding to his collection, and quite a number of his tricks had been based on old ideas which he had improved and brought up to date.

He had nothing but contempt for Barney, although he was prepared to use him to acquire the information which could be of service to his country. Barney was a traitor — a man who was prepared to sell secrets to the highest bidder for his own gain, irrespective of the harm such transactions could do his country. In Delmar's estimation, such a man was despicable.

He was asleep when the ring came at the front door bell. But he slept lightly, and it awoke him at once. As he got up and pulled on his dressing-gown, he glanced at the travelling clock on the little bedside table. It showed the time to be just after four o'clock. Who could be calling at such an hour?

He went out into the tiny hall and opened the front door. The man who was standing outside pushed his way quickly into the hall.

'Oh, it is you, my friend,' said Delmar as he recognized his visitor. 'Why do you come at this time?'

'I've brought what you wanted,' replied Barney.

Delmar pulled the dressing-gown closer round his lean body. 'Come into the sitting-room,' he said, and opened a door on the left. 'We can talk better in there, my friend.' He switched on the light and stood aside for Barney to enter.

'Now,' he said, shutting the door, 'you have got the information I asked for?'

Barney took the little roll of microfilm from his pocket and put it down on the table. 'There you are,' he answered.

Delmar picked it up. 'You can vouch that this is authentic?'

Barney nodded. 'I got it from the man I told you about,' he replied. 'He works at the Defence Ministry.'

'Why do you bring it at this hour? It would have been better to have brought it to the theatre.'

'I thought you were in a hurry for it.'

'And now you want your pound of flesh, yes?'

"That is not all I want. I need your help.'

'My help?' said Delmar. He looked at his visitor and nodded. 'I see. What can I do, my friend?'

'In a very few hours from now,' said Barney, 'there will be a hue and cry after me. They will know what I have been doing.' Rapidly he explained the situation, omitting, however, to say what he had done in the case of Slade. There was no need to tell this man about that. When he read of the death of Felton in the newspapers, he would conclude that it was suicide — as everyone else would. He might have his suspicions, but it was better that he shouldn't *know*.

'When I leave here, I am going to Scotland. I have a cottage on a deserted part of the Scottish coast. I want you to arrange for me to be picked up by air.'

'You are not asking much, my friend,'

said Delmar with one of his unpleasant smiles.

'You can do it,' retorted Barney. 'You can arrange with your country to land a small plane — there is a wide stretch of meadow near this cottage, big enough for a plane to land and take off.'

'It might be possible, my friend. But why should I do it? It was not part of our arrangement that I should be responsible for your safety if you were discovered.'

'You'll do it,' said Barney, and there was no mistaking the menace that underlay his tone, 'because on my safety depends your own. If I'm caught, it would only be a matter of hours before you would be arrested.'

'I see.' Delmar nodded, his snake-like eyes fixed on the other. "There is something in what you say, my friend.'

'I thought you'd understand.'

'It will take a little time to arrange. A week, perhaps.'

'That will suit me. The cottage is stocked with sufficient food to last that long. Nobody will know where I am. By the time they do, it will be too late.'

'Where do you want the plane to put you

down?'

'Anywhere on the continent that is suitable and safe. I can make my own way from there. Now, what about the payment for that?' Barney pointed to the film. 'I want ten thousand, cash.'

'I have not got it here,' said Delmar. 'You gave me no warning that you would be coming.'

'You said the money was waiting.'

'The money *is* waiting. It can be got first thing in the morning. You do not expect me to keep a sum like that here, my friend.'

'The morning will be too late,' said Barney. 'I shall be well on my way then.'

'I will arrange for it to be delivered to you if you give me the address.'

'How do I know I can trust you?' demanded Barney. 'You've got the film.'

Delmar shrugged his thin shoulders. 'You have it in your own hands, my friend. You can always betray me to the authorities if I fail to send this money.'

Barney seemed satisfied. 'You're right. And make no mistake — I would.'

'I seldom make mistakes, my friend,' murmured Delmar.

'I must go,' said Barney. 'It will be getting light in an hour.'

Delmar opened the door. 'You strike a hard bargain in every way,' he said as they passed out into the hall, 'but I will arrange everything as you wish.'

'You'd better,' said Barney.

13

In spite of the fact that a full description of the wanted man had been circulated throughout the country, no news of him came to hand. The Jaguar had been found abandoned in a side street on the outskirts of Northampton, but of its owner there was no trace.

'It looks as if he was heading north,' said Hallowes when he was told, 'but it may be a blind.'

The safe, when it was opened, revealed nothing; it was quite empty. Mrs. Grayle, by now convinced that her idol had feet of clay, was questioned again concerning anything she might know that would give a clue to Barney's present whereabouts, but she could tell them nothing. He had never spoken about himself at all. She had no idea whether he had any relations. Certainly none had ever visited him. She couldn't offer any help at all.

The woman who had been his secretary

at the office was equally void of useful information. There had been quite a number of people in and out of the offices, naturally, but she couldn't think of one who might have been more than a client. Her employer had taken one or two of them out sometimes in the evening, but it had been in the course of business. She couldn't suggest any woman with whom he might have been friendly.

Barney's bank manager and his lawyer were just as unproductive. They were both astounded to hear that their client was wanted by the police. They had both looked on him as a model of an honest, upright businessman. He had been meticulous in money matters. His account showed a reasonable balance at the bank, but nothing outstanding.

'All the money he made out of the secrets racket was in that safe, I'll bet,' commented Hallowes.

Barney's accountant was able to supply very little additional information. His client had been a director of a company that owned the block of offices and the mask shop. This company also held the lease of the premises which housed the Eldorado. There were three directors, including Barney, and the registered offices of the company were at the accountant's. The police sought out the other directors, but once again they met with a blank. They turned out to be respectable men who had seats on the boards of a number of other companies, mostly dealing with catering. They had believed, like the lawyer, the bank manager and the rest, that Barney was completely trustworthy.

'He seems to have fooled everybody,' grunted Hallowes. 'The only thing they don't remember about him was his halo!'

'He must have had contacts for disposing of the stuff he acquired,' said Slade. 'Perhaps there's a line there.'

'Perhaps — if we knew who they were,' grunted the superintendent sarcastically.

'Well, that office of his might have offered a very good meeting-place. He was always seeing people there. One or more of them needn't have been legitimate clients. They could have been the contacts, couldn't they?'

Hallowes took his pipe out of his mouth and regarded him thoughtfully. 'You know, that's not a bad idea of yours.'

'I have them sometimes.'

'You can follow it up. I'll get a list of all the people who saw Barney in the office, and you can check up on them. Not as a policeman. We'll think of a good character for you.'

Slade groaned. 'Why don't I keep my big mouth shut,' he said.

'How would it be,' said Hallowes, puffing out smoke like the Scotch Express, 'if you got hold of Lydia and became a double act? You know the kind of thing I mean — singers, dancers ...'

'I can't sing and I can't dance,' interrupted Slade.

'You wouldn't have to do either,' retorted Hallowes, 'You're out of work. You've been told that Barney is a good agent. That gives you an excuse to talk to these people.'

'And I suppose they're going to tell me that as an agent he's not much good, but if I want any secrets that's the place to buy 'em?'

'Just use your own judgement,' said Hallowes, ignoring the remark. 'Of course, it may not lead anywhere, but it's worth trying. This fellow has gone to ground somewhere, and it's more than likely that he's got someone helping him.'

Slade sighed resignedly. 'All right, I'll see what I can do. You get the list. We can eliminate quite a good number of people at once. The acts that are pretty well-known for a start.'

How wrong he was in this conclusion, he didn't find out until later.

★ ★ ★

The cottage Barney had prepared in readiness for just such an emergency as the one he now faced was situated near the edge of a cliff on one of the most isolated spots in northern Scotland. The nearest village was over three miles away, the nearest habitation a crofter's cottage over a quarter of a mile inland. The land was heather-covered grassland on which a few sheep grazed, and the cliffs descended sheer to the craggy rocks a hundred and fifty feet below.

The cottage itself was small, unsanitary, and built of stone. It was without comfort of any sort, although Barney, on one of the few occasions when he visited it, had installed a bed, an easy chair and an oil cooking-stove. There was only one room, and a kind of lean-to annex that served as a kitchen. Warmth was provided by a rough open fire that smoked badly until it had burned red. There was, however, plenty of fuel and food, tea, coffee and cigarettes, and Barney knew he could exist fairly well for a short period, which was all the cottage had ever been intended for.

In spite of these spartan conditions, he was feeling quite happy. In one of the cases that stood against the wall of the living-room was the equivalent of a fortune to satisfy any man. To this would be added the ten thousand from Delmar, and he had arranged for his means of getting out of the country. He could put up with a little inconvenience in the present when the future presented so many pleasant possibilities.

It was a wild night. On this coast the full force of the wind came sweeping in from the north; an icy, biting wind that rose to gale force and howled, screeching, round the cottage and lashed the sea to fury against the rocks below. Nature at its rawest could be found here.

The wind tonight was not as strong as it had been, but it was fairly fierce — too fierce for anyone to venture very far. But Barney had no intention of venturing anywhere. With cigarettes and a pot of coffee beside him, he lounged back in his comfortable chair and read one of the books that he had brought with him to pass the time. He was not a man who was very fond of reading, but here there was nothing else to do.

Presently, above the sound of the wind, he heard something that made him look up sharply. It was the faint sound of an engine.

He closed the book, put it down on the table, and got quickly to his feet. From the pocket of his jacket he took out an automatic — a twin of the one he had sent to Salvatori. Going over to the window, he lifted the rough blind at one corner and peered out into the darkness of the night.

He could see nothing. The wind came buffeting the house and drowned all other sounds but its own booming. But in the lull that followed, he heard the sound of the engine again. It was a petrol engine, and it was growing louder. There was somebody out there in the darkness coming towards the cottage. Another blustering gust of wind whirled away the sound; but now, faintly, he could see a single light moving along the cliff road. It was jerky and unsteady, and he guessed that it was attached to a motorcycle.

Who would be coming to the cottage on such a night? It could be a traveller going on to the next village. No — the light had turned off the cliff path and was advancing along the track that led directly to the cottage.

Barney's fingers closed more firmly round the butt of the little pistol. Surely they hadn't found him? He watched as the light came nearer and stopped at the gap in the low stone wall surrounding the cottage. The sound of the engine died away.

Barney dropped the edge of the blind and turned to face the door. There was no hall. The door of the room opened directly onto the unkempt garden.

There came a rap on the rusty iron knocker. He went over to the door and called: 'Who is it?'

'I have come from Delmar,' answered a

voice muffled by the heavy door. 'Open up and let me in.'

Barney put away the pistol and pulled back the bolts. He ought to have guessed who it would be, he thought, as he unfastened the stout chain. He had been expecting this ever since he had reached the cottage.

The force of the wind almost blew the door out of his hand as he lifted the latch, and a figure in shining black oilskins almost fell into the room. Barney forced the door shut against the wind; and the lamp, which had almost gone out in the draught, leapt up again, nickered, and began to burn steadily once more.

The visitor was shaking his oilskin hat and loosening the cape at his throat. He was a small, dark-featured man with a thin face and restless eyes.

'You've brought me something?' asked Barney, and the dark man nodded. From under his cape he produced a package wrapped in brown paper. 'This is the money,' he said, and his voice was harsh and unfriendly. 'I also have a message for you. The plane will pick you up tomorrow night. You must be ready at midnight. You will have to watch for the landing. It will carry a blue light. If you are not ready, it will take off again without you. It will not wait.'

'I'll be ready,' said Barney. He tore off the wrapping from the parcel. Inside there were packets of notes, ten bundles of them. 'You'd better take those oilskins off,' he said, 'and get warm. It's a nasty night. How far have you come?'

'Not very far,' said the other. 'I won't stay. I'll be getting back.'

'Have a drink before you go,' said Barney. He picked up a bottle of Haig, but the messenger shook his head.

'No,' he answered curtly. 'I must go.'

Barney shrugged his shoulders. If the man didn't wish to be friendly, it was his business. He seemed to be rather an uncouth sort of fellow. But he'd brought the money and delivered his message. That was all that mattered. 'A good stiff tot would help to keep the cold out,' he said. 'But if you'd rather not ... '

'I must go,' the other repeated, and re-buttoned the cape at his throat. 'Don't forget — midnight tomorrow.'

'I shan't forget,' said Barney. He went over to the door and opened it. There was a lull in the wind and it was less difficult. The man pulled on his hat and stepped past him.

'Good night, and thanks,' said Barney.

The other grunted something in reply and walked out into the darkness. Barney heard the engine of the motorcycle splutter into life. The headlamp, barely a spark, moved round towards the cliff road. As he closed the door, he heard the engine rev up, and then a gust of wind blew the sound away.

He came back to the warmth of the fire. On the table lay the pile of notes, and he surveyed it with satisfaction. Delmar had been true to his promise. The plane would pick him up tomorrow night, and that would be that. Barney would be away from this draughty, isolated cottage, in the sunshine of a foreign country — safe and with nothing to do but seek enjoyment with the fortune he was taking with him.

He sat down and let his mind drift into a pleasant contemplation of the future.

* * *

Superintendent Hallowes provided Slade with a complete list of all the clients who had used Barney's Variety Agency to look after their contracts. It was a formidable list to start with, but with the assistance of a reliable theatrical agent, and his own common sense, Slade succeeded in reducing it to fourteen possible suspects — people who might be employed as contacts by some foreign power. These fourteen were further reduced to nine after inquiries revealed that the others couldn't possibly be anything but what they seemed.

As Mario and Lydia, adagio dancers, Slade and Lydia began a systematic round of night clubs, theatres, and the larger cinemas — all the various places where these nine people had contracts. They were, they said, looking for a sole agent to handle their act. They had heard that so-and-so, the particular person they were talking to, had found Barney very good. What could they tell them about him? Was he reliable? Did he get the contracts? They had had agents before but they hadn't proved satisfactory.

They found the majority of the people they talked to both friendly and helpful. Their attitude towards Barney was mixed. Some declared he was good, some that he wasn't. Some suggested the names of other agents, and two offered to arrange an audition for them with the management that they themselves were working for.

'And that would be fatal,' remarked Slade, over a cup of coffee in a coffee bar, to Lydia. 'I know as much about adagio dancing as a baby elephant in the African jungle.'

She laughed. 'That applies to me too,' she said. 'We haven't got very far, have we?'

'The whole idea wasn't very brilliant. Actually, I never expected Hallowes to take it seriously.'

'I'm not at all sure that he has. I caught a humorous twinkle in his eye when we were talking to him about it.'

'Well, I certainly don't think that any of the people we've seen up to now are anything but straightforward,' said Slade. 'That leaves the acrobats with Bartlet's Circus, and The Great Delmar.'

'We'll try him first. I suppose there's no

news of Barney?'

Slade shook his head. 'He seems to have vanished completely. I suppose he's hiding up somewhere, waiting for an opportunity to slip out of the country.'

'I think what we're doing is just a waste of time,' Lydia declared. 'Is it likely that if there's a foreign agent among these people, he or she is going to give themselves away? They'd be far too clever.'

'That wasn't entirely the idea,' said Slade. 'It was that if we found anyone who might — I repeat, *might* — be a possibility, the counter-espionage people would get to work and follow it up. But I haven't found anyone who remotely warrants further investigation.'

'We might be doing a worse job, I guess' said Lydia. 'That's something to be thankful for.'

As a preliminary to interviewing The Great Delmar, they saw his show. It was the usual elaborate conjuring entertainment in an exotic setting. There was no doubt that Delmar was good. Quite a number of the illusions he performed were original. He included a variation on the vanishing trick in his programme that was completely new.

A glass coffin was brought onto the stage and placed upon two chromium steel trestles. Two members of the audience were invited to come up and examine it. Delmar, clad in a black skin-tight costume, got into the coffin and lay down at full length. His two female assistants put on the glass lid to the coffin, and it was sealed in four places by the members of the audience who had been invited to the stage. Now came the presentation of the trick which made it different from any other of its kind. Instead of the coffin with Delmar inside being covered by a cloth, there was a great flash of light and a billow of smoke. Only for a single instant did this obscure the glass coffin from view; but when it cleared away, Delmar had vanished — the glass coffin was empty! The seals were examined and found to be unbroken. During the applause which followed, a hearse drawn by a black pony came slowly onto the stage. As it stopped in the centre, Delmar stepped out and bowed. That was the culmination of his act. The heavy plush curtains swept down, and Delmar came through them to take his call.

'That's the best illusion I've ever seen,' declared Slade as he and Lydia made their way round to the stage door.

'How did he do it?' Lydia mused.

'Don't ask me. It's probably very simple when you know how. Most of these tricks are. But how it's done, I can't imagine. Usually they cover the cabinet, or whatever it is, with a cloth; but this is new.'

The stage-door keeper took their names when they asked to see Delmar, and went away. After a short interval he returned to say that Mr. Delmar would see them. They found the conjuror sitting at his dressing-table, sipping a cup of coffee. He had not yet started to remove his make-up.

'You wished to see me?' he asked. 'You are dancers?'

'Yes,' said Slade. He explained the reason for their call, as he had done on so many other occasions. But this time, at the mention of Barney's name, he saw a sudden wary expression come into the eyes of the man he was talking to. He had seen that expression before too often not to know what it meant. Delmar had something to hide.

'I have always found Barney's Agency very efficient, but I understand that he has gone out of business,' said Delmar. 'Is that not so, my friend?'

'You mean it's closed down?' asked Slade in well-simulated surprise.

'Did you not know?' said Delmar.

'I should hardly have come here with my partner to inquire what you thought of him as an agent if I had,' answered Slade.

'It is surprising that you did not know. If you are so anxious to know about the Barney Agency, I find it extraordinary that you did not make inquiries at the offices.'

'We wished to find out if it was any good first,' put in Lydia. 'We didn't want to go there until we had.'

'Your methods are unusual,' said the conjuror. 'It would seem useless to bother further, since the business is no longer in existence. I am sorry that you have had so much trouble for nothing.'

The tone was a dismissal. They left Delmar beginning to remove his make-up and exited the theatre. 'I think,' said Slade as they walked up the street, 'that we may have found something interesting. That man knows something. Did you see his expression when I mentioned Barney?' Lydia nodded. 'The Great Delmar will repay investigation, I think. I'll report to Hallowes, and he can get counter-espionage onto it.'

'Well, I'm glad we haven't been entirely wasting our time,' said Lydia.

'Don't count your chickens,' warned Slade. 'This is only a possible line. There may be nothing in it after all.'

* * *

Delmar received a visitor later that night at his small flat off the Tottenham Court Road. The visitor was a stout man whose round, good-humoured face would have been recognized by quite a number of people who regularly frequented a certain nightclub in the region of Piccadilly, for he was the bland and smiling head waiter who welcomed them so efficiently. But he was not smiling as he talked rapidly to Delmar, and by the time he had finished, nor was his host.

'You are sure of this, my friend?' asked

the conjuror anxiously.

'There is no doubt,' answered the other seriously. 'I received the information from one of our contacts a short while ago. I came to tell you at once.'

'There cannot possibly be any mistake?'

The stout man shook his head. 'They would not make a mistake over so serious a matter. It has been checked very carefully — of that you can rest assured.'

'What are we going to do, my friend?' muttered Delmar.

'It is your responsibility. You arranged these things.'

'In complete good faith.' Delmar got up and paced the small room with his long, thin hands clasped behind his back, his face puckered in thought. Presently he stopped. 'All is not lost,' he said. 'An idea has come to me. We can retrieve the situation if we act at once. You are able to get in touch with the head of our group without delay?'

'I could arrange for a message to be delivered in a few hours.'

'Good! Then this is what must be done. The present arrangements must be carried out, but there will be this difference ... ' He lowered his voice and spoke quickly in his own language.

The stout man listened, nodding now and again in approval. 'It is an excellent plan,' he said when Delmar had finished. 'I will see that it is put into operation at once.'

'It is up to them to decide what they do — afterwards. I think, my friend, something very drastic should happen, eh?'

'It will. You need have no fear about that. We do not like being made fools of.' The stout man went over to the door. 'I will see that everything is done as you suggest. It will meet with approval, of that I am sure.'

After his visitor had gone, Delmar sat down and picked up the old book he had been reading before he had been interrupted. It was a book on card tricks he had picked up that morning in a bookshop in Charing Cross Road.

That he had sent a man to his death, or possibly something worse, worried him not at all. He was not worthy of any consideration. Such people, in Delmar's estimation, should be destroyed with as little compunction as one would destroy vermin.

Salvatori sat in the office of the Eldorado, his face grey and anxious. Since he had been released from the police station after his questioning by Inspector Mason, he had scarcely known a second's peace of mind. At any moment he expected to be arrested and charged with the murder of Clint. So far his fears had not been realized.

He had seen nothing of Snow. That scared man had disappeared completely, at least from the vicinity of the restaurant. Nor had he heard anything from the man who had for so long ruled his life. He, too, had vanished. Salvatori was not sorry about this. He would have been glad if he never heard anything from him again. All he wished now was that he could be released from this apprehension of impending arrest that hung over him, and be allowed to continue to attend to his job of running the Eldorado. He was a restaurateur at heart. He always had been.

The door opened and he looked up. Detective-Inspector Mason came in, followed by the sergeant who had accompanied him on the night of Vanya's murder.

'I 'ad nothing to do with it,' declared Salvatori before either of the police officers could speak. 'That pistol was never mine. I swear to you that I 'ad never seen it before. It is the truth that I tell you.'

'We haven't come about that,' interrupted Mason. 'I am not charging you with the murder of Clint. The post-mortem revealed considerable bruising of the body, and we have come to the conclusion that the man was shot in the offices of Barney's Agency and afterwards thrown into the yard.'

'You believe that I am innocent?' broke in Salvatori. 'I told you — the pistol was sent to me; it was a frame-up.'

'We agree with that,' said Mason. 'At the same time, I have to warn you that anything you say will be taken down in writing and may be used as evidence hereafter.'

Salvatori stared at him, his eyes bulging. 'But,' he cried, 'if you are not arresting me for that … ?'

'I am taking you into custody and charging you with being an accessory, both before and after the fact, to the murder of

Vanya,' said Mason sternly. 'Get your coat.'

Salvatori tried to speak. His lips moved but no sound issued from his dry throat. He swayed for a moment, put out a fat hand to steady himself, and fell forward across the desk.

With an exclamation, Mason went to him and stooped over him. After a brief examination, he turned to the sergeant. 'Go and telephone for a doctor,' he said crisply. 'I think he's had a stroke.'

★　★　★

Rodney Barney looked at his watch. It was twenty minutes to twelve. The plane should arrive soon, and he was ready for it. The two suitcases were locked and waiting. It wouldn't be long now before he was speeding on his way to safety.

The night was dark but the wind had dropped. He could hear the faint murmur of the sea on the rocks below the cliff, but the angry roar of the previous night had gone.

He took a last look round the cottage. It had served its purpose as a temporary resting place before he began his new life — a life of ease and luxury that only wealth could give him. And he had money in abundance. It would be easy to sell the diamonds; they were negotiable in any country in the world. The ten thousand pounds would be enough to last him until he could arrange a sale. There would be no need to rush things. He would have ample time to find the best market.

He went over to the side table and poured out a drink from the bottle of Haig and swallowed it neat. The spirit sent a flood of warmth through his veins and enhanced the feeling of well-being that pervaded him. Very soon now, he would be exchanging this desolate and deserted coast for the warmth of sunshine and the gaiety of a new country. He hadn't, as yet, made up his mind where he would settle. Perhaps for a while he would travel from place to place, until he found the exact spot that most appealed to him. He had no ties — nothing to stop him doing what he pleased.

He picked up his suitcases, opened the door, and stepped out into the darkness of the night. Although the wind had dropped, it was very cold, and he was glad of the heavy overcoat he wore. Except for the sound of the sea, it was very still. He looked up into the black void of the sky. There must be a veil of thin cloud, for he could see no sign of stars. The plane would be carrying a blue light, the messenger had said. He would hear the sound of the engine, in any case.

He walked out through the gap in the low stone wall and looked about him. Would the plane be able to land near the cottage, or would he have to go some distance? The long, flat stretch of clifftop offered plenty of space if the pilot could judge his distance. But it would be difficult in the dark. If anything should go wrong with the landing — if the undercarriage should get damaged and they couldn't take off? What would happen then? A wave of uneasiness flowed over Barney. Or supposing there was a hitch and the plane didn't turn up? He shook off his pessimism. Everything would be all right. It had *got* to be.

He looked at the illuminated dial of his watch. It was exactly midnight.

His eyes searched the blackness above him and his ears strained to catch the first sound of the engine. But he could neither see nor hear anything.

Five minutes past the hour.

What had happened? Had something occurred to delay the plane? Perhaps there had been engine trouble, and the pilot had been forced to turn back or make a landing somewhere? The feeling of well-being now fled, leaving him anxious and apprehensive. He looked back at the vague outline of the cottage. Would he have to go back?

And then, faintly, he heard the sound from somewhere over the sea — the rhythmic throb of an engine. His heart began to beat faster and his hopes soared. He was a fool to have expected that the plane could be dead on time. Of course, the hour had only been approximate. They wanted to make sure that he would be ready so that there should be no waiting. After all, they were risking a certain amount in coming at all.

The sound of the plane was getting louder. Barney could not see any sign of it as yet, but it was drawing rapidly nearer.

Presently, he judged that it must be almost overhead. He stared up into the sky but could still see nothing. By the sound of the engine, the plane seemed to be circling above him.

And then he saw it — a tiny spark of blue light that suddenly flashed out of the darkness. It grew bigger, and the noise of the engine became a roar. The blue light was coming lower and lower, and he saw it moving towards him smoothly at first, and with a bouncing motion as the plane touched down. The sound of the engine died to silence, and the blue light, distinguishable now as coming from the top of the cockpit, came to a halt.

Barney ran towards it. A man was getting out of the small cabin. He swung himself to the ground and turned as Barney reached the side of the plane.

'You are Barney?' The voice was harsh and guttural, with a strong foreign accent.

'Yes,' answered Barney. 'That was a nice landing.'

'You are ready — get in,' said the man curtly.

'I've got to fetch my suitcases,' said

Barney. 'I won't be a —'

'I come,' broke in the man. 'Show me.' He followed Barney to the place where he had left the bags. Without comment, he picked them up and started back to the plane.

When they reached it, Barney saw that there was a second man leaning out of the cockpit cabin. The first man handed up the suitcases, one at a time, and the man in the cabin took them and stowed them away inside.

'Now you,' said the man on the ground.

Barney put his foot on the wing and, with the help of the man inside the cabin, was able to scramble aboard. There wasn't a lot of room in the small cabin, but he was able to squeeze into the seat which the man indicated. This man was evidently the pilot, for he was seated at the controls.

The other man climbed quickly in, and the pilot said something to him in a language that Barney did not understand. The man nodded, and the pilot pressed a button. The engine spluttered to life and settled into a deafening roar. The little plane shuddered and began to move slowly forward. It gathered speed, bumping over the ground, and then the bumping suddenly ceased and they were climbing upward smoothly as the plane became airborne.

Looking out of the side window of the cabin, Barney could see nothing, only blackness. Whether they were over land or sea, he couldn't tell. But he was away. His heart sang. A few more hours and the darkness would be gone.

'Where are you making for?' he asked the man beside him, but he received no answer. He tried again. 'I suppose,' he said, 'you have arranged where you are going to land me?' The man beside him nodded. 'Where is it?' inquired Barney. 'Not that I mind a great deal. Anywhere on the continent will suit me.'

'You will see,' answered the man. He was staring straight ahead, obviously not inclined to answer questions.

Barney shrugged his shoulders. If they didn't want to talk, it was all the same to him. There were lights now, faintly visible below. He watched them, like tiny pinpoints, spread out on a velvet carpet.

The little plane droned on.

He must have fallen asleep, for the next thing he remembered was opening his eyes to see the sun rising. Below, he could see very little. There was a thin mist that seemed to cover everything.

'Where are we?' he inquired.

'We are nearly there,' grunted the man beside him.

'We've been travelling for a long time,' said Barney. 'It's dawn. Where are we now?'

It was the pilot who replied. 'It can make no difference to you where we are,' he said, 'You will go where you are told.'

A tinge of uneasiness ran through Barney. What was the meaning of this attitude? 'I don't understand,' he said. 'You were supposed to set me down on the continent. No fixed place was mentioned, but I expected — '

'That was before certain information reached us,' answered the man sitting next to him. 'We relied on your good faith. We have been betrayed.'

Barney looked at him in astonishment. 'I don't know what you mean,' he said. 'How have I betrayed you, as you call it?'

'What do *you* call it?' asked the other.

'But I don't know what you're talking about. What have I done?'

'You sold us worthless information,' replied the man beside him.

'Worthless information?'

'It is useless trying to pretend you do not know,' put in the pilot. 'The information you sold to our agent, Delmar, was faked. Luckily, it was discovered in time. You will not be able to profit from your deception.'

Barney felt a sensation like a lump of ice inside him. Felton had swindled him. The information he had supplied as authentic was trumped up for the purpose.

'I assure you —' he began, but the man beside him cut him short.

'You will have an opportunity of talking when we reach our destination,' he said. 'Until then, keep silent.'

'Where are you taking me?'

'You are being taken to headquarters,' answered the pilot. 'The money will be confiscated and you will be questioned. It will then be decided how you will be punished.'

'You can't do this,' cried the frightened man. 'I acted in good faith. It was not my fault if I was deceived — '

'Perhaps, if you can prove that, your sentence will be lenient,' said the man beside him. 'Otherwise … ' The pause he made was more significant than anything he could have said.

Barney felt a cold sweat break out on his forehead, though it was hot in the confined atmosphere of the little cabin. All his dreams of a happy future in ease and luxury toppled about his head like the falling of a house of cards. He would be stripped of everything, and be lucky, into the bargain, if he escaped with his life.

*   *   *

The counter-espionage agents were delighted with the tip concerning Delmar. They got extremely busy, with the result that two weeks later, the magician was arrested one morning as he was leaving his flat off the Tottenham Court Road.

He accepted the situation philosophically. 'I was afraid, my friend,' he remarked to the man who charged him, 'that this would happen one day.'

Hallowes had an interview with him in his cell. 'What,' asked the superintendent, 'has happened to this man, Rodney Barney? Do you know where he is?'

Delmar gave one of his least pleasant smiles. 'If he is still alive, he is probably undergoing an extremely unpleasant ordeal. I would not like to change places with him, my friend.'

'The man who sold him that information was one of my men,' said the superintendent. 'You are blaming Barney for something he didn't do.'

'No matter. Nothing could happen to him that he doesn't deserve, my friend.' Hallowes was inclined to agree with him.

'He's right,' remarked Slade when he heard about it later. 'Barney was one of the worst characters I've ever come up against, and I've met a few.'

'You are going to meet a few more,' said Hallowes. 'I've got a new job for you, and I want you to start at once.'

Slade groaned. 'What is it this time?'

'You will become a rag-and-bone dealer,'

answered the superintendent calmly. 'There has been a gigantic fraud perpetrated in scrap metal.'

'What am I supposed to do — count the scraps?'

'That will be up to you,' said Hallowes, carefully filling his pipe. 'If that's the only way you can find out who is at the bottom of these frauds, then I rely on you to do your duty.'

Books by Gerald Verner
in the Linford Mystery Library:

THE LAST WARNING
DENE OF THE SECRET SERVICE
THE NURSERY RHYME MURDERS
TERROR TOWER
THE CLEVERNESS OF MR. BUDD
THE SEVEN LAMPS
THEY WALK IN DARKNESS
THE HEEL OF ACHILLES
DEAD SECRET
MR. BUDD STEPS IN
THE RETURN OF MR. BUDD
MR. BUDD AGAIN
QUEER FACE
THE CRIMSON RAMBLERS
GHOST HOUSE
THE ANGEL
DEATH SET IN DIAMONDS
THE CLUE OF THE GREEN CANDLE
THE 'Q' SQUAD
MR. BUDD INVESTIGATES
THE RIVER HOUSE MYSTERY
NOOSE FOR A LADY
THE FACELESS ONES
GRIM DEATH

MURDER IN MANUSCRIPT
THE GLASS ARROW
THE THIRD KEY
THE ROYAL FLUSH MURDERS
THE SQUEALER
MR. WHIPPLE EXPLAINS
THE SEVEN CLUES
THE CHAINED MAN
THE HOUSE OF THE GOAT
THE FOOTBALL POOL MURDERS
THE HAND OF FEAR
SORCERER'S HOUSE
THE HANGMAN
THE CON MAN
MISTER BIG
THE JOCKEY
THE SILVER HORSESHOE
THE TUDOR GARDEN MYSTERY
THE SHOW MUST GO ON
SINISTER HOUSE
THE WITCHES' MOON
ALIAS THE GHOST
THE LADY OF DOOM
THE BLACK HUNCHBACK
PHANTOM HOLLOW
WHITE WIG

with Chris Verner:

THE BIG FELLOW

We do hope that you have enjoyed reading this large print book.

Did you know that all of our titles are available for purchase?

We publish a wide range of high quality large print books including:
Romances, Mysteries, Classics
General Fiction
Non Fiction and Westerns

Special interest titles available in large print are:
The Little Oxford Dictionary
Music Book, Song Book
Hymn Book, Service Book

Also available from us courtesy of Oxford University Press:
Young Readers' Dictionary
(large print edition)
Young Readers' Thesaurus
(large print edition)

For further information or a free brochure, please contact us at:
Ulverscroft Large Print Books Ltd.,
The Green, Bradgate Road, Anstey,
Leicester, LE7 7FU, England.
Tel: (00 44) **0116 236 4325**
Fax: (00 44) **0116 234 0205**

Other titles in the
Linford Mystery Library:

DEATH WARRIORS

Denis Hughes

When geologist and big game hunter Rex Brandon sets off into the African jungle to prospect for a rare mineral, he is prepared for danger — two previous expeditions on the same mission mysteriously disappeared, never to return. But Brandon little realises what horrors his own safari will be exposed to . . . He must deal with the treachery and desertion of his own men, hunt a gorilla gone rogue, and most terrifyingly of all, face an attack by ghostly warriors in the Valley of Devils . . .

PHANTOM HOLLOW

Gerald Verner

When Tony Frost and his colleague Jack Denton arrive for a holiday at Monk's Lodge, an ancient cottage deep in the Somerset countryside, they are immediately warned off by the local villagers and a message scrawled in crimson across a windowpane: 'THERE IS DANGER. GO WHILE YOU CAN!' Tony invites his friend, the famous dramatist and criminologist Trevor Lowe, to come and help — but the investigation takes a sinister turn when the dead body of a missing estate agent is found behind a locked door in the cottage . . .